SUMMER AT
END HOUSE

DIANA F. GREEN

LUTTERWORTH PRESS

CAMBRIDGE

Lutterworth Press
7 All Saints' Passage
Cambridge CB2 3LS

British Library Cataloguing in Publication Data

Green, Diana F.
    Summer at end house.
    I. Title
    823'.914[J] PZ7

ISBN 0-7188-2640-X

Copyright © 1975 Lutterworth Press

First Published 1975
First paperback edition 1987

The poem *The Gardener* which appears on
pages 62-5 is copyright by Diana F. Green
and reproduced by kind permission.

All rights reserved. No part of this publication may be reproduced,
stored in a retrieval system, or transmitted in any form or by any means,
electronic, mechanical, photocopying, recording, or otherwise, without the prior
permission in writing of the publisher.

Printed by
The Guernsey Press Co. Ltd.,
Guernsey, Channel Islands.

Contents

To

my niece

JOCELYN

with the hope that when she is old enough
to read this book, she will enjoy it

Briony Looks for Adventure

BRIONY stood in the garden of End House and breathed a long, slow sigh of contentment. There were several reasons for this. To begin with, it was the first full week of the long summer holiday from school. Secondly, they had recently moved house. Moving was not her parents' idea of bliss, but it was a glorious adventure for Briony. Then, lastly, they had moved to End House, which was nice enough in itself. But it also had a simply wonderful garden.

Briony was very fond of gardening. Where they had lived before, on a council housing estate, there had only been what her brother called "a large pocket handkerchief". Her father had had an allotment, though, and ever since she was very small, he had taken her there with him and had taught her all he could.

When Briony was very small, she had found it fun to trundle away piles of Dad's weeds in her toy wheelbarrow, and to pick bunches of bright flowers for her mother to arrange at home. But as she grew older, she found fun in quite a different sort of way; learning what to do so that things grew. It gave her great satisfaction to know that she had helped to tend the vegetables which they ate for dinner; it was a great thrill to pick flowers for her mother which she had actually sown and watered and looked after.

"Do you like it, darling?" her mother had asked, rather anxiously, on their first visit to End House. And Briony had replied rapturously:

"Oh, Mother, it's *heavenly!*"

"You haven't even been inside the house," her brother Mark objected. "So how can you say?"

"I don't need to go inside the house," Briony had retorted. "Look at the garden!"

"Yes, *look* at the garden!" her father had echoed ruefully. "It doesn't look as though anyone had done anything *except* look at it for years and years. It's terribly neglected."

"That's all right. Think what fun we'll have, discovering what there is!" Briony said happily.

"We can see what there is—*weeds*," Mark said disparagingly. "Better rent it out as pasture for someone's cows. Or concrete the whole thing over."

"We shan't do either, you dreadful boy," his mother said quickly. "Don't forget that this is the first proper garden your father has ever had. He'll have no end of a time."

"Rather him than me!" Mark retorted. "Will

this house be big enough for me to have a room to study, away from all the kids' racket?"

"Yes, but you will have to share with Briony," his mother warned him. "She will have home-work, too."

"But *we* shan't," Simon said. He gave his mother an angelic smile. "Me an' Sarah can play and play——"

"At least there is plenty of room here, without you having to go out into the road," his mother said thankfully. "Mark, there is a little room in the front which I thought would do for your study. Come and see if you like it."

They had gone off together, leaving the three younger ones to roam the garden at will, though the twins had soon run off, hand in hand, on their own tour of exploration. Not that Briony minded. She had spent a perfectly blissful afternoon wandering round the garden, and gave her father a somewhat incoherent account of her findings later.

"—A huge lawn, Dad—or it will be once it's mown and the edges are properly trimmed—currant bushes of all sorts—even a great big patch of strawberries somewhere. And there are those lovely apple trees all along one side. But the bottom's just *wild*—it's *lovely*!"

"Lovely, is it, chicken? I don't know. It will

need an awful lot of work," Mr. Hunter said seriously. "Still, if we all have a go, we should make something of it between us."

This was the chance Briony had been waiting for. She said eagerly, "Dad, *couldn't* I have a piece for my own? To do as I like with? *Please?*"

"Well, that depends what you want to do with it," Mr. Hunter said cautiously. "And had you any particular piece in mind?"

"Yes; some of the wild bit at the bottom of the garden. There would be enough room to make a lovely rockery—and I've always wanted a rockery," Briony said wistfully. "And could we have a pool—a little one? If the rock plants hung over towards the water, you would get the colours twice over and it looks gorgeous—*please*, Dad!"

Her father had been doubtful, but had finally agreed. A pond lining was easily bought, and he promised that if Briony helped to reclaim the bottom part of the garden, he would help to make her rockery.

"But I shan't do all the work for you," he warned her, "though I'll do a lot of the heavy digging, of course. But the dreary round of weeding will be all yours. And next year, if I can see that you have really put some effort into it, and this isn't just a whim, you shall have your pond."

Dad had already done some heavy digging, and Mark, rather to Briony's surprise, had also helped for an hour or two. And she had spent several afternoons, getting hot and filthy in the process, of doing the dreary but necessary work of weeding. Indeed, she had spent nearly all her spare time out there, and it was her mother's insistence that she was now, clean and tidy, ready to set off for Nether Walden, the little market town.

"You can do with an afternoon off, darling. Go and find the library; we have already arranged for the transfer of our tickets, so you can have some books out if you see any you like. And look around for a bit. You've stuck at the garden very well and a change will do you good."

Briony thought this was a good idea, and was quite willing to catch the bus and set off. It would be fun to explore on her own.

It *was* fun, but after the first hour, Briony began to feel rather lonely, and wish that Jennifer and Pauline, her two special friends, were with her now. They would be able to come and stay later, but not this year, because of the move. And anyway, Briony had already had a picture postcard from Pauline, who had gone to a Guide Camp, while Jennifer—lucky thing! thought Briony enviously—was probably this minute on a plane to Italy with her parents.

Two books were quickly found in the library, and then Briony wandered on to Market Square, where she found plenty to interest her, for Saturday was market day and there were all sorts of stall set up, and some of them were really exciting, especially the pets' stall. But there was also one which was really a surprise, for it sold Bibles and books about Jesus. And although there were also pencils and rubbers, they all had verses from the Bible stamped on them. There were two stall-holders: a white-haired old man with very blue eyes and a jolly smile, and a girl who Briony thought must be about sixteen or seventeen. She was quite happy to let Briony browse through an exciting story which she had found. And when Briony regretfully put the book down, she said:

"See you again perhaps? God bless you."

Briony didn't quite know what to say to that, but it seemed rude to say nothing, so she just said, "Goodbye."

As she turned away from the stall, she noticed two girls who were standing staring at her. One was taller than she was, with long fair hair, and one was shorter than she was, with short brown hair, but they both looked as though they were her own age.

"Go *on*, Heather!" the dark one said, in a sort

of urgent whisper, but the girl with the fair hair replied, in the same tones:

"Jessamy, I just *can't*! *You* do it!"

Briony looked at them curiously, and was just going to go on her way, when the two looked at each other and then turned to Briony and said:

"Excuse me, please——" in a breathless sort of way.

Briony looked surprised. "Did you want me?"

"Yes," both girls said together. Then they stopped. Then they looked at each other and then they looked at Briony. And then they all, including Briony, started to giggle.

The brown-haired girl recovered first. "Look—move—we're blocking the gangway," she said. "But—oh dear! this isn't a bit as we'd planned."

"But what *had* you planned?" demanded Briony.

"We wanted—we want to talk to you. Will you come over here, where there's more room, so that we can?"

Completely mystified, and nearly forgetting her shopping, Briony obediently followed them over to a convenient seat under some trees. Then the fair girl tried again.

"We want to talk to you," she began, "because we have a wonderful Friend, and we want to introduce you."

"Perhaps you know Him, too?" the other girl said eagerly. "You might. But we had agreed that we would ask the next girl who stopped at the stall, and it was you, and we felt awful, but we'd agreed——"

Poor Briony looked more bewildered than ever and despite themselves, all three giggled again.

"We're doing this awfully badly," the dark girl said. "We don't even know your name. But I'm Jessamy Marchant and this is Heather Jones. Now, what's your name?"

"Briony Hunter," Briony said, still rather dazed. "But why should you want me to meet your friends when you don't even know me? And what does that stall have to do with it? And why does it make you feel awful to talk to me?"

"One at a time," Jessamy begged. "It sounds even worse when you fire it all out like that! I know it all sounds frightfully queer, and I'm sorry, but I will try and explain. We aren't crackers or anything, truly."

"All right, you aren't crackers," Briony said patiently. "But please *do* explain! And who is this friend?"

"It's Jesus," Heather said simply. "We wanted to tell you that Jesus really is alive. But perhaps you knew?"

Heather and Jessamy

BRIONY was so very much surprised by this unusual annoucement that for a few minutes she just sat and stared. Jesus was alive?

"Didn't you know?" Heather asked hopefully, and Briony looked at her with puzzled dark eyes.

"Didn't I know?" she repeated wonderingly. "About Jesus?"

"Yes. You do know who He was?" Jessamy asked.

But this was more than Briony could stand.

"Of *course* I know who Jesus was!" she said indignantly. "He lived about two thousand years ago and said He was the Son of God. So the Jews killed Him—on Good Friday. *Everyone* knows that!"

"They don't seem to," Heather argued. "Some people we've talked to are frightfully surprised to think that we think that it matters now."

Briony thought it was rather surprising herself, but the two strange girls were so much in earnest that she didn't like to say so. However, it must have shown on her face, because they looked at each other. Then Jessamy said:

"You said that He died on Good Friday,
Briony, but why didn't you go on? What about
Easter Sunday?"

"What about it?" Briony asked, puzzled.

"Don't you know what happened?"

"Well, yes," Briony said slowly. "He came
alive again—I *think*!"

But if Briony was uncertain, it was more than
the other two were.

"He *did* come alive again!" Jessamy said
triumphantly. "He was truly the Son of God and
the devil just couldn't win, and death couldn't
hold Him. He rose from the dead—and He is
alive today!"

"Oh." Briony looked curiously at them. "You
seem very excited about it. I didn't think it
mattered very much. After all, it's not as if it
makes much difference today."

"But it *does* make a difference," Jessamy
argued. "And yes, we *are* excited about it.
Because we have met Jesus for ourselves—we
know He is alive and He loves us—and what could
be more tremendous than *that*?"

"I don't know," Briony said helplessly. "I've
never thought about it."

"We thought you might not have," Heather
agreed. "We didn't for a long time, but then we
really met Jesus—and it makes all the difference

and we want to tell other people about it, too, in case they don't know."

"What sort of difference does it make?" Briony asked.

"All sorts," Heather said simply. "There are so many horrid things in the world; so many people are hungry and haven't got homes and so on, and are sad and frightened. It can make you awfully unhappy if you think about it. But when you know that Jesus cares much more than you do, it helps. And besides, when you know that you belong to Him, you know that He will take you to heaven one day and then you will see the answer to all the things you couldn't understand."

"That doesn't help the people who are lonely or homeless now, though," Briony protested.

"Yes, it does," Heather said eagerly. "Because, you see, from the time that Jesus was on earth, people have always gone and told other people about Him, and doctors and nurses and teachers and people like that have gone, too. So the ones that can be helped are helped, and the ones who are ill and perhaps won't get better can learn about Jesus and go to live with Him when they die. Christian missionaries have always been the —the first in the field—to help other people, because they love Jesus."

"Yes," Jessamy agreed, as Heather paused for

breath. "And Jesus said that if people wanted to show how much they loved Him, they were to go and do things for other people. Besides, it's so *splendid* to know Jesus; you can't *help* going out and telling."

"That's why we're here," Heather added. "Because we're all right—I mean, we have nice homes and parents who love us and look after us, and proper food to eat and nice clothes to wear— *and* schools to go to, though that doesn't always seem so good! But what I'm trying to say is that life is wonderful, anyway, but when you get to know Jesus, it's as if—as if——"

"—as if you had been living in a black and white world, but when Jesus comes, He puts all the colours in," Jessamy added, and Heather beamed.

"That's just about right! Do you see?"

"I don't know," Briony said honestly. "I tell you, I've never thought about it before. But I do see what you mean about the colours; at least, I think I do! But what does that have to do with you talking to me?"

"I don't wonder you are puzzled," Heather said sympathetically. "We did rather throw it all at you, didn't we? But it's quite simple. We got to know Jesus for ourselves, and it made us so happy that we wanted to tell other people about it. So we asked if we could. And Pat—she leads our Bible class—said why didn't we start telling our friends and other girls of our own age, because we knew we aren't clever and not much good at explaining. And she said that the Holy Spirit would help us, if we were sincere."

"You weren't scared, though, were you?" Briony asked curiously.

"Oh, we were!" Heather said fervently. "Dreadfully! But we knew we had to start, so we thought we would talk to the next girl of our own age who stopped at the gospel stall——"

"—and no one did for simply ages, and we were quite glad," Jessamy grinned. "Then you came! And we felt simply dreadful, especially as you stood there for so long, but we knew we simply had to wait and ask you. So we did!"

"I see," Briony said thoughtfully. "But you know, I really don't see how you actually got to know Jesus. It isn't as though He were here, is it?"

"But He *is* here!" Jessamy cried. "That's just it! When He ascended to heaven, He promised to send His Holy Spirit to teach us about Him, and He does just that. And you get to know Him by talking to Him—in prayer—and by listening, too, and by reading the Bible, which tells us about His people, and what He did on earth, and what the

beginning of the church was like. Look here!
We've been talking for ages and it's hot and I'm
thirsty. Shall we go into the café and have a
drink?"

They all agreed that this was a good idea and
were soon sitting round a table in the window of
"The Copper Kettle".

"You can get lovely iced orangeade here,"
Heather said.

So they all had iced orangeade and sat looking
out at the busy street and got to know one another
a bit better.

"Where do you live?" Heather asked, when
they had quenched the worst of their thirst. "Do
you live in Nether Walden? We do."

"No; in High Walden," Briony said.
"Actually, we only came there a week ago, so this
is the first time that I've been here; on my own, I
mean. I came in the car with the others, to do
some shopping."

"Whereabouts are you living?" Jessamy asked.
"Are you in the bit that's nearly in Nether
Walden, or in the villagey bit?"

"I suppose you'd call it 'the villagey bit',"
Briony said, rather doubtfully. "It's right at the
end of the main road and there's a sort of village
green and a duckpond. The house itself is called
End House."

"Why?" asked Heather.

"Because it *is*," Briony explained. "There are lots of houses along the road and then there's us. And the garden stretches out for a long way—it's a super garden!—and then there's the road, and then the village green."

"It sounds nice," Heather said. "We both live quite near to here, but we have often been out to High Walden on our bikes. There are woods near there and in the spring they're just thick with primroses and violets."

"That sounds lovely," Briony agreed. "Will you show me where?"

"Rather! You can see the place—it's nice to walk there any time, and of course it's gorgeous in the autumn, when the leaves are turning colour. What about your family? Have you any brothers and sisters, or is there just you?"

"No; there's Mark, who's fourteen and then there's me and I'm just twelve. Then there are Simon and Sarah; they're twins and just six. How about you?"

"I've one brother, Bruce. He's nine," Jessamy said.

"And I've two sisters—Anne's eighteen and Kathryn's fifteen," Heather said. "So I'm the youngest. And we're both twelve, too."

"So now we know a bit about each other,"

Jessamy said with satisfaction. "Where are you going to school, Briony? Do you know yet?"

"Yes; Peter Street Comprehensive," Briony said. "But please don't let's talk about school just yet! The holidays have only just begun."

"All right, we won't if you'd rather not," Heather agreed easily. "Though I believe it's not too bad. We're both going there, too, so we're sure to see a bit of each other, anyway. But it would be fun if we could make friends first. I'd like to."

"So would I."

There was a pause after this and then Briony said, "I still don't believe that Jesus is interested in me."

"Well He is, the Bible says so," Jessamy said stoutly. "And He's a special Friend because He did what no other friend could do for you; He bought you when He died on Calvary."

"And why should I need buying?" demanded Briony. "I haven't done anything very bad."

"It's not so much what you've *done* as what you *are*," Heather said. "And you're human, like everyone else. So, instead of doing what God wants, you're bound to do as *you* want—and then you get into difficulties."

"Oh, I can see that," Briony said fervently. "Mother says so often, 'You wouldn't listen to me;

you thought you knew best, so don't grumble about the consequences.' Do you mean like that?"

"Exactly like that," Jessamy agreed. "You see, Briony, when we do things we shouldn't, they go wrong and we can't make them right again. But Jesus *can*. So when a person turns to Him and says 'I'm sorry about how bad I am, but there is nothing I can do about it,' He will take that person into the presence of God and say 'Don't look at this human being and how bad he is; I saved him from all that and paid for him when I died. Just look at me instead.' "

"And Jesus is perfect, so there can be no blame attached to us," Heather said.

"Yes, I see," Briony said slowly. "I see."

And she did, but it was all so new and confusing and muddling that she didn't quite know what to think next. But the other two seemed to realise how she felt, because they both started talking about something else, and by the time they left the café they were chattering away like old friends.

"Shall we meet you another time? We'd like to," Heather said, as Briony began to think it was time she went to find her bus.

"I'd like to, as well," Briony agreed. "Have you got a telephone? You see, as we have only just come to the house, there are still lots of things to do and Mother and Dad expect us to help. And I don't know what they have planned for different days."

"We haven't a phone but Heather has," Jessamy said promptly. "Give us your number, Briony, and we'll ring you to arrange something. Would you like to come to tea one day?"

"I'd love to, but I must ask Mother first," Briony said prudently. "If you ring later this evening, I'll have told Mother and Dad about meeting you, and I can have asked them by then if there is anything special they want me to do on any special day. Will that be all right?"

"That will be fine. Come round to us, later, Jess, and then we'll ring up together," Heather suggested.

"All right. I've promised to give Bruce his tea and put him to bed for Mother, but I can come after that. It's just the early part of the evening that I have promised to be there."

The two friends escorted Briony to her bus-stop and saw her on to the bus and then made their way home, talking hard about their meeting and Briony's response.

Briony, too, had plenty to think about. Indeed, she was intent on her thoughts so much that she missed the stop when she should have got off and

found herself with an extra walk to get home.
But she soon stopped minding that for, turning a
corner, she found herself facing a house which had
quite the loveliest garden she had ever seen in her
life.

Smooth green lawns sloped down to borders
which were a riot of colour and bloom. Rose
bushes, holding choice blooms of every imaginable
colour, formed a column leading to the front door.
The hedges were neatly trimmed; in fact the
whole garden spoke of the loving care which it
received. But it was the piece of garden at the
back of the house which took Briony's attention.

For there was another lawn, looking exactly like
a stretch of green velvet, and it ended in a water
garden. And the water garden ended in a rockery.
Yes, a rockery. And the purple aubretia and
yellow alyssum hung over the water, and the
colour was reflected so that it gave twice the
pleasure. In fact, it was the garden of Briony's
dreams, and she was so enthralled that she forgot
all she had ever been told about good manners
and hung over the wall, frankly staring. And she
stayed rooted to the spot until she heard a sharp
voice saying:

"Well, little girl? And what do *you* want?"

3

Another Meeting

MISS LOMAX was a very old, very energetic and very sharp-tongued old lady. She was the sort of person who has very strong and pronounced likes and dislikes. And because she was so old and particular—but also because she was very lonely, and so was rather sad—she only had two things in her life which she really loved. One was Ginger Bob, her big cat. The other was her garden.

There were many things which Miss Lomax disliked, but one of the things she most disliked was children. She had never forgotten or forgiven the fact that she had rescued Ginger Bob as a tiny kitten from some boys who were trying to drown him. And she had never forgotten or forgiven, either, the day that two boys had come into her garden to fetch their cricket ball. They had been in the middle of a most exciting game and Roger Smeaton had hit the ball much further than anyone would have thought possible. So it had gone into Miss Lomax's garden, and the fielder had gone with him to fetch it. Which was

quite natural, except that he had unfortunately
not asked Miss Lomax first. If he had, she would
have grumbled, but being reasonable—as older
people are, in their own way—she would have
let Roger fetch it willingly enough. But he had
not and, bending down, had been startled by an
angry voice. It was so unexpected that he had
overbalanced on to some of Miss Lomax's care-
fully erected cloches. They were ruined, but what
was even worse, so were the tiny plants which
Miss Lomax had grown from seedlings and
protected with such loving care, against the
rigours of the weather. So, naturally, with this in
mind, when Miss Lomax saw a strange child
leaning heavily over her garden wall, her first
reaction was to shout loudly, and also very
angrily.

Briony came out of her haze of delight with
the knowledge that somebody, somewhere, was
not pleased. And she looked up, blushing
guiltily, and found herself facing a very irate old
lady.

"What do you want?" Miss Lomax repeated
sharply.

"Want? Nothing," Briony said, sounding
rather surprised. "I was just looking."

"Oh? Why?" Miss Lomax demanded.
"What's wrong with my garden?"

That brought Briony sharply back into reality.

"Oh, nothing!" she exclaimed fervently. "*Wrong* with it—why, it is just the most beautiful garden which I have ever seen in my life!"

She was so transparently sincere that Miss Lomax had to believe her. She looked sharply at the girl for a moment.

"Hm," she said eventually. "So you like my garden?"

Briony could think of no adequate reply to this. She just nodded.

"Like gardens, do you?" Then—as Briony nodded again—"Do you do any gardening yourself?"

"Yes, but not much until now," Briony said. Then something in the forbidding face of the old lady urged her to go on——

"You see, we never had a proper garden before. Only an allotment, and that was sometimes too far away for me to go to. But now we have come to live at End House—do you know it?"

"Naturally," Miss Lomax said sharply. "Having lived here for the greater part of my life, it would indeed be strange, were I *not* familiar with all the houses round about. End House, eh? Well"—and there was a certain grim satisfaction in her voice—"there is plenty of work to be done *there*!"

"Yes," Briony agreed. "Dad said that it didn't look as if anyone had ever done anything except *look* at it for years."

"And he was quite right," Miss Lomax said tartly. "Let the place go to rack and ruin; shameful, I call it. Nothing that a bit of hard work wouldn't have coped with easily, though."

"We're going to work hard on it," Briony said eagerly. "In fact, we already *have*. Dad and Mark—he's my elder brother—have done some digging, and I've done a lot of weeding. That's one reason why I came out today. Mummy said I needed a change."

"She sounds a sensible young woman," Miss Lomax observed, and Briony laughed out loud.

"Why, Mummy isn't *young*. She's quite *old*; well over forty. That's old, isn't it?"

"Terribly," Miss Lomax said, with a grim smile. "Tell me, you curious child, how old do you think *I* am?"

Briony didn't much like being referred to as a "curious child" and she was still not sure whether or not Miss Lomax was cross or not. There was nothing in the grim face to reassure her, but she smiled, as she said hopefully.

"Ninety?", and was rewarded by a frosty smile coming over the lined face.

"Thank you for nothing, miss! I'm seventy-nine now, but I still have my health and strength. Well, if you like the garden so much, you had better come in and see it. You can't get a proper view from that wall."

"I—I—oh, thank you!" Briony said rapturously. And indeed, the next half hour was solid delight, for Miss Lomax, once she realised that she had a kindred spirit, became quite animated as they strolled round the garden.

"This," Briony said wistfully, as they approached the rockery and water garden, "is what I like most of all. It is what I want to have at home." And she told Miss Lomax of the rockery which she was to build and the pool which her father had promised she should have, if she kept her word and really cared for her garden.

"So you like my rockery, do you?" Miss Lomax commented, looking at Briony's delighted face with satisfied eyes.

"Yes, I do. And you have done what *I* was going to do; made the plants hang over the water so you have them twice over."

"Hmph!" said Miss Lomax and she looked thoughtfully at Briony as they walked round.

When the tour was well on the way, Briony heaved a sigh.

"It's all so perfect. Do you really do it all yourself?" She eyed Miss Lomax with respect.

"Most of it. Young Jim from the farm comes and does any digging which needs doing; I'm finding it rather difficult to do all I'd like to in that direction."

All the time they were walking round, Miss Lomax poured out information at such a rate that Briony's head was spinning. As they neared the house, she said:

"You must be in a complete muddle after all that. Would you care to come in and have a cup of tea with me?"

Briony, thus drawn back to the present, gave a guilty start.

"I'd love to, but I don't think I ought," she said. "Mummy will have been expecting me at home for some time now."

"Quite right. I'm glad that some mothers these days still bother about what their children get up to," Miss Lomax returned. "Run along then, child, by all means."

"Er—may I come again?" Briony asked, rather shyly, and a spark came into the old lady's tired eyes.

"If you would like to, of course. Do. I'm always here."

"Thank you very much," Briony said. "I'd

love to come. And then I can tell you how we are getting on with *our* garden."

"You can. But somehow, I think it will be a long time before I need fear any competition," Miss Lomax said dryly, and Briony laughed.

"Oh, it will be ages. But I'd love to come and see you, anyway, Miss—er—Miss——"

"Lomax. Beatrice Lomax."

"And I'm Briony Hunter. How do you do?" Briony said, belatedly, and Miss Lomax gave the first proper smile that Briony had seen.

"I do extremely well, thank you very much! Now don't stay, child, if your mother is expecting you. The garden will still be here another day."

"Goodbye, then. And thank you."

And then Briony went running and jumping along the road, and burst into End House, where her mother looked up with a sigh of relief from the pudding which she was taking out of the oven.

"Is that you, Briony? You're very late, darling. I was beginning to get worried. Tea's nearly ready. Wash at the kitchen sink and then you can tell me about your afternoon at the same time," Mrs. Hunter suggested.

"I met Heather and Jessamy—because they'd seen me reading at the stall in the market—and they wanted to tell me that Jesus was alive, and did I know? And I said I did, but I didn't think it was anything to do with me—and they said it was—oh, Mummy, have you got any pumice stone? I seem to have got something awfully messy on me—and so we had orangeade and talked, but we'd talked a bit before—and they explained how Jesus was a friend to them and they said He could be to me, and I want to think about it, because it's rather surprising. Then we talked some more, and then I started to come home. Only I was so busy thinking that I didn't see the bus had come past our stop, so I went right down to where Heather and Jessamy call 'the villagey bit' and when I was walking back, I saw the most glorious garden—is there a towel, or shall I have to go to the bathroom?"

"There's one here," Mrs. Hunter said, smiling as she handed over the kitchen towel. "Where was this glorious garden? Is it open to the public? If so, you and Dad had better go along one Sunday afternoon."

"Oh, it's not *that* sort of garden," Briony protested. "It's just someone's garden, belonging to their home, except that it's lovelier than you could ever imagine. Just think, Mummy; a proper water garden in it, too."

"Goodness me! Where is it?"

"At the end of the village. I forget the name of the house, but you can't mistake the garden. It

belongs to Miss Lomax," Briony explained.
"She's ever so old—seventy-nine—but she does
all the work herself, except that someone helps
her with the digging. And she knows an awful lot
about it, Mummy. She knew the name of every
single plant and flower and the sort of care each
one needed; you know, if it liked a lot of water, or
to be in the shade, or things like that. She's really
very clever. And she invited me to go again."

"That will be nice, then, won't it?" Mrs.
Hunter said cheerfully. "Now, tea is just about
ready, so perhaps you would help to carry things
in. Oh, by the way, did you get the shopping?"

"Yes. I chucked it all down in the lobby. Is
that all right?" Briony asked, and her mother
smiled.

"It will do for the time being, anyway. Give
Mark a call, will you? Simon and Sarah are
ready; Dad has been amusing them while I was
getting the tea."

In spite of her ice-cream and orangeade earlier
in the afternoon, Briony was quite ready for her
mother's cold pie and salad, and a delicious hot
lemon pudding to follow. Mr. Hunter had taken
the twins out for a drive in the afternoon and they
had seen a man who sold puppies, and in the
exciting discussion about whether they would or
would not have a puppy of their own one day,

Briony's two meetings were forgotten. But later, when she was washing up—she and Mark took turns every day—she told her father all about the meeting with Miss Lomax and he was as interested as she had expected he would be.

"I think I know the house you mean, and I agree about the garden; it's a picture. But you'll find that out here, where we are so near to real country, people do have nice gardens and take a real pride in them. I expect that they have fruit and flower shows in Nether Walden. You would like to go to those."

"Yes, I would," Briony agreed. "Can we show anything, Dad?" Her father grinned. "Not this year! Unless there is a class for thistles. Oh, and we've a splendid show of groundsel!"

Briony was still giggling over this idea when the telephone rang and Mark, who had answered it, shouted:

"Telephone for you, kid."

"I wish he wouldn't call me that. I'm not much younger than he is," Briony objected.

But it was, of course, Heather and Jessamy who were telephoning, and so she soon forgot to be cross. Instead, she set about arranging things with her new friends.

Mark, looking into the room which the family had dubbed "the study", was much amused to find Briony seated in lonely state at the table, peering intently over one book, while others were piled up beside her. Most of them were the books the family had about gardening. But one was a Bible.

More About Miss Lomax

BEFORE another meeting had passed, Briony, Heather and Jessamy had become firm friends. And as Heather put it, they "fitted together", in spite of the fact that they were all quite different. Or maybe it was because of it.

Briony, cheerful and generous, was always willing to help others, which made her at times overcome her natural diffidence. Jessamy was quick and clever, but inclined to be both sharp-tongued and impatient; in complete contrast to shy, gentle, artistic Heather.

The three had many conversations about the Christian faith and the other two were always willing to lend Briony their books, and were thrilled to see the interest of their new friend.

It was the first Saturday after her meeting with them, and Briony was diligently trimming the edges of the newly mown lawn when there was a click at the gate, and she saw her mother coming in with the shopping. And when they were sitting together in the shade, enjoying a cold drink, Mrs. Hunter said:

"Listen, Bri! I heard something in the village

shop just now which might interest you. You
know you came in last Saturday and told us about
the old lady with the beautiful garden?"

"Miss Lomax," agreed Briony. "Why?"

"Because it seems that you are rather a
privileged person. Apparently your Miss Lomax
doesn't have friends—hardly ever goes out,
except to do necessary shopping—and doesn't
like children. Of course, she sees people like the
postman and the baker, and her doctor calls
occasionally to make sure that she is all right,
but she certainly never invites anyone to go and
see her. So Mrs. Wyngate at the shop told me.
She was *most* surprised when she heard about
your invitation."

"Oh," Briony said. She was surprised, too.
Certainly, Miss Lomax had spoken sharply at
first, and she had seemed a little gruff once or
twice. Yet if she really disliked children, why was
she so keen to answer Briony's ready flow of
questions? Why did she tell her that she was
welcome to return whenever she liked? It was
very strange.

There was no solution to the puzzle, though,
and Briony went back to her trimming and
thought no more about it for the time being. Her
mother thought about it, though, and mentioned
it to her husband when they were alone.

"What do you think? Should we try and stop her going any more?"

Mr. Hunter considered for a a few moments.

"No!" he said eventually. "I don't think we should. After all, this Miss Lomax sounds as though she can be quite a formidable old lady. I think we can safely trust her to look after herself. As for Briony, personally, I think she has managed rather well. It must be the garden which made a link between them, and it certainly sounds as though the old lady *needs* a friend. Good for Briony, *I* say!"

So they left it like that, and on Monday morning Briony once more set off for Cypress House, whistling cheerfully, as she often did. She was beginning to know people in the district, and they usually smiled or waved and said "Hullo" when they saw her. But in spite of herself, she felt rather nervous as she walked up one of the beautifully kept paths, by the stiff cypress trees— for once, the name suited the house, she thought. She rang the bell and there was a pause. Then Briony heard steps—surprisingly quick ones, she thought, for Briony was very observant for her age. Then the door opened, in a stiff sort of way—as though it wasn't used to being opened very much—and there Miss Lomax was.

"Hullo, I've come," Briony said. "Is it all right?"

"Good morning, Briony Hunter," Miss Lomax said, with a quirk of her mouth which could almost have been a smile. "I'm glad you kept your word and came to see me. How is the garden growing?"

"The *weeds* are doing splendidly," said Briony at once, and Miss Lomax smiled properly at that.

"No breaks in the jungle anywhere?"

"Oh yes. We have cleared all the borders round the lawns, and the lawns themselves have been mown; Dad did that and I trimmed the edges, and they look very nice. Now we've started on the hedges, and I'm weeding the paths, but it's a slow job."

"Yes. And very dull," Miss Lomax said. "Come in, child."

The house seemed very dark after the bright sunshine outside, but although Briony looked round curiously, there was little chance to see anything, for she was led straight out into a place which looked like a cross between a greenhouse and a sitting room. It was made entirely of glass, but there was a table and a couple of chairs. Apart from that, it was full of flowering pot plants.

Miss Lomax watched Briony's face as she took it in.

"Like it, do you?" she asked casually.

"Very much," Briony said enthusiastically. "Is it a conservatory?"

"More or less," Miss Lomax admitted. "I call it my garden room. When the mornings are bright and sunny, as it was today, for instance, I bring my breakfast out here."

"That must be fun," Briony agreed. "We have tea in the garden sometimes. Now, I mean. We couldn't really where we lived before, because it was an industrial estate, and it somehow seemed cleaner inside."

"I don't doubt it *was* cleaner inside," Miss Lomax said dryly. "Sit down, child."

Briony sat obediently, and Miss Lomax followed suit. Then there was quite a pause before Miss Lomax said:

"And how are your plans going?"

"For my garden? Not much more than plans, because there is so much ground to clear. But Miss Lomax, if I get stuck over my gardening, would you—well—would you help me?"

"If I can assist you at any time, I shall of course be pleased to do so," Miss Lomax said gravely. "The first and best thing to tell you is that nothing worthwhile can ever be achieved, in gardening as much as anything else, without thought, preparation and hard work. Is the basis of the rock garden already there?"

"No," Briony admitted. "But there's the remains of a wall which Dad thought we might be able to use."

"Yes, that sounds splendid. It would blend in with the house, too, which is important in a small garden. Then, before you begin, it might be a good idea to make a plan of the sort of thing you want to do. If you can't draw, a diagram will do just as well. For instance, do you want to concentrate on one particular colour, and blend as many shades as you can? Do you want rare plants only? Or a hotch-potch?"

"Oh dear," Briony said, her face falling. "I didn't think there was so much to it."

"Even if you aren't going to go in for show-growing or anything like that, you need to do a bit of thinking before you plunge in," Miss Lomax pointed out. "Why not settle for the hotch-potch? That way you get plenty of variety, and if something springs up which you didn't know about, you can always pretend that you meant it to happen like that!"

Briony brightened again.

"I don't want to start off very grandly and then——"

"Fizzle out? No, of course you don't. And you

don't want people to say you've bitten off more than you can chew, either," Miss Lomax said shrewdly. "And by the way, if you are going to be looking around for plants, go easy on the wild flowers, won't you? Everyone has a duty to protect the wild flowers so that everyone can enjoy them."

Miss Lomax went on to speak of famous gardens —and some unknown to most—that she had visited. Briony listened entranced, until she was disturbed by the sudden touch of something against her hand. With a start, she looked down, and saw a large ginger cat, which was staring at her in a very suspicious manner.

"That's Ginger Bob," Miss Lomax said calmly. "Did he frighten you?"

"No," Briony said. "It was just that I didn't expect anything like that."

She stretched out a hand, but Miss Lomax shook her head.

"I shouldn't try to touch him. He doesn't like strangers."

The words had barely been spoken before Ginger Bob suddenly leapt lightly into Briony's lap. There, he curled round, and soon lay quietly.

"Well, I never did!" Miss Lomax said, astonished. "I have never known Ginger Bob be so friendly with a stranger—and certainly not anyone so young. He dislikes them—with good reason."

"Why?" Briony asked, and the old lady's voice became sharp with anger, as she said:

"I was out walking in the village when I saw two or three boys—lads of about your age—messing about near the duck pond. They had Ginger Bob—he was quite a young kitten. They were tormenting him very cruelly and tried to drown him. They certainly caused him a lot of unnecessary suffering. So I took him home with me, after making sure that the police would deal with those young thugs. Now he is around five years old. He's a good cat. And he's company."

"Don't you get lonely, all by yourself?" Briony ventured to ask, but Miss Lomax's face seemed to shut up as she said:

"No, indeed. We do very well together, Ginger Bob and I."

As if he heard his name, the ginger cat woke and yawned. Then, with delicate movements of his paw, he began to wash his face. Briony watched in delight and was quite sorry when he leapt lightly off her lap and streaked through the open door. She stood up to watch him, and her attention was caught by a framed picture by the door. It had obviously been done by hand, and

Briony exclaimed in delight over the flowers which bordered it, as well as the beautiful lettering.

"Did you do this, Miss Lomax?"

"What? Oh, that illumination? I painted it—and did the lettering—but I didn't write the words," Miss Lomax said, getting up to look over Briony's shoulder. "Don't you know them?"

"I don't think I have ever seen them before," Briony said.

"It's a carol—Dutch—and comes from the seventeenth century. There is music to it—also Dutch," Miss Lomax informed her, and watched as Briony began to read.

"King Jesus hath a garden,
    full of divers flowers,
Where I go culling posies gay,
    all times and hours.
There naught is heard but Paradise bird,
Harp, dulcimer, lute.
With cymbal, trump and tymbal,
And the tender, soothing flute."

"That's funny—but rather nice," Briony pronounced. "It reminds me of what someone was telling me the other day."

"And what was that, may I ask?"

Briony looked from the illumination back to her hostess with puzzled eyes.

"They told me that Jesus is alive—and could be my Friend if I wanted Him to be. Did you know about that?"

"What makes you ask that?" Miss Lomax asked tartly.

"I just wondered. You see, you had these verses. And they're about Jesus, aren't they?"

"Yes, I suppose so. Well, I won't keep you. You'll want to be meeting your friends, I don't doubt."

Briony was about to say that she wasn't going to do anything special, but then she realized that Miss Lomax didn't really want her there any longer, so she got up meekly and prepared to leave.

"May I come again?" she asked timidly, and Miss Lomax, who had been frowning out into the garden, looked up with a start.

"Come again? Yes, of course you may. Haven't I already said so?"

"I'll look forward to it," Briony assured her. Then, as she noticed that Miss Lomax really looked like an old lady today, she said quickly:

"I'll see myself out if you like, Miss Lomax."

"Very well then. Goodbye."

"Goodbye." And Briony rather soberly made her way through the hall out into the sunshine.

"Good morning, young lady! Do you want to see Miss Lomax?"

"What?" Briony looked round, puzzled. Then she noticed that a short and cheery man in a tweed suit was making his way up the path, with a small black case in his hand.

"Oh! I didn't see you for a minute, the sun's so bright. No, I've just *been* to see her."

"You have?" The man looked startled. "How did *that* happen?"

"Miss Lomax invited me," Briony said, surprised that such an obvious reply hadn't occurred to him.

"Well, well. So the age of miracles is not yet past!"

Briony was more puzzled than ever.

"What did you say?" she asked politely.

"I said—well, never mind what I said. Did you come for anything special? Miss Lomax isn't ill, is she?"

"Oh no. Or, not that I know of," Briony said. "She seemed tired just now, but that was all. No, she invited me to look over her garden the other day, and today she invited me to go back again any time."

"What is your name?" the man demanded.

"Briony Hunter. Is there anything wrong?" Briony asked, rather alarmed by all these questions.

"Wrong? Good heavens, no! It's just that you

are the first person who has called on Miss Lomax
in a friendly way for a very long time. And to be
invited back is a real accomplishment."

"I like Miss Lomax," Briony told him. He
looked pleased.

"Good. I think she can do with a friend. I'm
her doctor, by the way, Dr. Meadows."

"Oh! Then you're *our* doctor, too," Briony
said. "We've just come to live at End House."

"End House—of course! I thought the name
'Hunter' had a familiar ring to it," Dr. Meadows
said. "Well, nice to meet you, Briony. I must go
and see Miss Lomax now."

"So that's *two* friends Miss Lomax will have
had to see her today," Briony said, pleased, and
he chuckled.

"I don't think I'm classed in that august
category. More likely to be counted as a Necessary Evil! Good day to you," and the friendly
doctor hurried up to the front door, smiling,
leaving Briony to stroll back to End House.

"It seems to me," she thought, as she went in
the gate, "that if there *is* anything in this business
about Jesus being our Friend, that when I've
found out for myself, I'd better make sure I tell
Miss Lomax all about it. Because she seems to be
a bit short on friends!"

The Village Mystery

" . . . but *how* does it make a difference, asking Jesus to be your Friend? Are *you* different?"

"No. Only wish I was!" Jessamy said gloomily. "I've got a fearful temper, and if things upset me, I just go off whizz-bang—like a rocket!"

Briony giggled. It tickled her to think of Jessamy firing off. But although Jessamy laughed, too, she soon looked serious again.

"It's all very well, but it bothered me, because I thought if I behaved like that, I couldn't possibly be a Christian. It was Pat who showed me the difference between deliberate sin, and falling into sin. And the fact that I feel sorry now when it happens, when before I used to feel that I was in the right, proves that there is a difference in me, too."

"Do you agree, too?" Briony asked Heather.

"Yes, though in a different way from Jess. I think the biggest difference Jesus has made is inside, where it doesn't show. I mean"—as Briony stared—"don't you ever get scared about things? Such awful things happen, and sometimes it seems that there is no one in control at all.

Now, when something awful happens, or I read about terrible things in the papers or something, I can go to God and trust Him with them, because, as it says in one of the songs we sing 'He's got the whole wide world in His hands'."

"There's a song in Miss Lomax's garden room which made me think a bit," Briony said eagerly. " 'King Jesus hath a garden', it's called. Could someone's life be like a garden?"

"Oh yes, I think that's a good comparison," Heather said. "Pat's got a poem about Jesus acting as a Gardener in someone's life. We could ask her to lend it to us, if you like?"

"I would; very much," Briony said emphatically.

"Isn't gardening a bit slow?" asked live-wire Jessamy, but Briony shook her head.

"It takes time, but what doesn't that's worthwhile? Can you imagine anyone winning at Wimbledon, for instance, without lots of practice?"

"No," Jessamy admitted. "Who is Miss Lomax?"

"You know. The old lady who lives in Nether Walden; the one with the gorgeous garden."

"Not Cypress House?"

"Yes, that's right. Why?"

"Because—goodness me, Briony! No one goes

to see Miss Lomax! She doesn't like people. All she likes is her garden—and her old cat."

"Ginger Bob. And he isn't all that old," Briony said indignantly. "That's the second time people have tried to make out that Miss Lomax isn't friendly. And I think people are horrible about her!"

And Briony, hot and flushed, looked resentfully at her friends. They looked uncomfortably at each other. Then Heather said:

"Sorry, Briony! We didn't mean to upset you. It's just that for years and years Miss Lomax has refused to see anyone. And it's a bit of a mystery because she *used* to have friends. Now she doesn't—and no one knows why."

"I can see why you call her a mystery," Briony admitted, mollified at this contrite apology. "But she truly is very nice. I certainly want to go on seeing her. In fact, I'm going again this week, when I've drawn up my plan."

Mark, busily cleaning his bicycle, was most surprised to see Briony solemnly crawling round the garden with her mother's tape measure.

"Whatever are you doing? Prospecting?"

"Not exactly. I'm trying to draw a plan of my garden, and I thought I ought to measure it up," Briony explained, and Mark grinned.

"A good thing you only have a patch; not a twelve-acre field! What do you want a plan for?"

"Miss Lomax said it would be a good idea," Briony said, and he screwed up his face.

"Miss Lomax—oh, that old dame in the village. Everyone round here seems to think she is a bit nuts."

"Well, she isn't, so there!" Briony said crossly, and Mark grinned again.

"Keep cool! No one could be nuts and grow flowers like she does. I came home that way after I heard you raving about it and for once, you haven't exaggerated! It's great."

"Lovely, isn't it?" Briony said happily. "I hope mine will be, too."

Miss Lomax, when Briony presented her plan, agreed that she could make a start.

"Why," she said, as Briony looked down, "don't you want to begin? I thought you were longing to make your own garden."

"I was," Briony confessed. "But now it's come to it, I don't think I'm so keen, after all."

"Why? In case you do something wrong?"

"Ye-es," Briony admitted.

Miss Lomax gave a snort.

"That's nonsense, child! How do you think the history of the human race would read, if everyone

had felt the same about every undertaking,
whether small or great?"

"I should think it might have been a bit
different."

"I very much doubt if we would have lasted this
long," Miss Lomax said tartly. "Listen, Briony
Hunter. If there is something which you very
much want to do, then for goodness' sake go
ahead and do it. There is every likelihood that
you will make mistakes; human beings are always
likely to do that, you know. So just don't bother
about it. You are young enough to start again."

"But suppose I muck it up?" asked Briony.

"Then grub it all up and start again!" Miss
Lomax said sharply. "Goodness gracious, child!
It isn't lack of knowledge which is holding you
back. It's human respect—which is nothing more
than pride. And that's nothing to be glad about.
Go and get on with it!"

Briony blushed scarlet. "You're quite right,"
she said, in a small voice. "I want it to be really
gorgeous and in my dreams it *is*! But the actual
thing might not match up to it."

"The reality rarely comes up to the dream,"
Miss Lomax said dryly. "But it is usually more
satisfactory. You will find that, as you get older,
though I don't expect you to believe me. Why
should you?"

"Why shouldn't I? You are a lot older than me and I'm sure you know a lot about things," Briony said warmly. "And it's awfully good to give me your time like this."

It was Miss Lomax's turn to change colour, for she became pink with pleasure. But when she spoke, her voice was as gruff as usual.

"I've told you that you are welcome here and I am glad to do anything which will help your garden along. There is just one thing I would like to ask from you and that is a promise that if, for some reason, you should call and find me not around, you won't go anywhere about on your own. It's so easy to cause damage without meaning to, especially in somewhere like the greenhouse, for example."

"Oh no; I wouldn't dream of looking round on my own," Briony assured her. "If you weren't here, I'd be disappointed, but I'd go away and come again another time."

Miss Lomax looked relieved.

"Thank you. I don't want you to feel that I'm just a fussy old woman, but my garden is very precious to me."

"I don't wonder at it," Briony agreed. "By the way, where's Ginger Bob? I haven't seen him today."

"Probably gone for a walk round the village,"

Miss Lomax said. "He goes off for hours when he is in the mood. But he is always here when it's meal-time; never you fear! What have you been doing with yourself lately?"

Briony immediately launched into a vivid description of her explorations into Walden Woods, and Miss Lomax nodded.

"A beautiful place, I agree. Did you find the swimming hole?"

"We found a pool," Briony said doubtfully. "Is it the one you mean? In the middle of a coppice, in a clearing?"

"No; although I know the one you found," Miss Lomax said. "The swimming hole is deep in the wood; you might not be allowed to go that far, these days. But it's a lovely natural pool for bathing. My brothers used to bathe there all through the summer."

"Did you have a lot of brothers?" Briony asked. It was the first time Miss Lomax had mentioned any family.

"Three," Miss Lomax said, with a reminiscent chuckle. "Derek and Roger were older than I was and Bernard was a little younger. But we were all very good friends. Then we had a sister, Lydia, but she was the oldest of us all."

"Lydia Lomax," Briony said, trying it out. "That sounds a nice name. What are they

all doing now? Do any of them live near
by?"

"No," Miss Lomax said shortly. "They're all
dead."

"What, *all* of them? Oh, I *am* sorry!" Briony
said earnestly. "And I'm even sorrier, because it
must make you awfully lonely sometimes."

"I haven't complained, have I?" Miss Lomax
asked.

"No. But you must be. I wish there was some
way of helping," Briony said. She sounded so
genuinely concerned that Miss Lomax bit back
the sharp reply that she hadn't asked for anyone's
pity, least of all that of someone young enough to
be her grand-daughter.

"Oh, I'm all right. No need to bother your
young head about me," she said.

"What about you? Have you any brothers and
sisters?"

Briony was very fond of her family and she soon
launched into an enthusiastic account of all they
had done since they moved, and of the fun they
had as a family. And then Briony babbled
happily on about her new friends, Heather and
Jessamy, and how they were enjoying each other's
company.

"But you know, Miss Lomax," she said
seriously. "I'm really beginning to think that

what they said is right and that the best friend of all is the Lord Jesus. He's always there, you see."

"Considering that I knew about Him before you were born, or even thought of," Miss Lomax said tartly, "then I might say that I do see!"

"I'm sorry," Briony said contritely. "I get a bit carried away sometimes. But you see, although you've known about it for years I've only just started to think about it, so it's all new to me and I find it rather exciting. Don't you think it's exciting, when the God Who made all the world and everyone in it, bothers about people like you and me?"

Miss Lomax was so quiet for such a long time after this that Briony began to be afraid that she had offended her old friend. She got up to go, and that roused Miss Lomax from her own thoughts.

"Time you went and did some work round your garden, is it? Well, don't work too hard. And come along again when you like and tell me how it's getting along."

"I will," Briony promised, and skipped off down the trim paths. And Miss Lomax went out into her beautiful garden and stared, unseeingly for once, at the bright borders.

For years now she had been in isolation and so had not heard the things of God. For years she had been protected by her silence; protected by the barriers she had raised against others and which they, in their turn, had erected against her. But suddenly those barriers had been knocked aside and she could only see Briony's clear, honest eyes and hear the wonder in her young voice, as again she heard those words——

"Don't you think it's exciting when God— bothers about people like you and me?"

Yes, God might conceivably bother about Briony, with her happy, open attitude to life, and her youth which made beginnings so easy. But how could He show that He bothered about a lonely old woman, who was shunned by those around her. A friend? A friend who was "always there". Oh, that would be wonderful, Miss Lomax thought, with a sudden ache in her heart. But what was the use? It was all right for these young people to get excited about things like that, but she was no longer young, and of use to no one.

At that moment in her thoughts, the orange cat came stalking majestically up the garden path. He rubbed against her legs and purred loudly. But instead of saying "Just in time for dinner, I see!" as she usually did, his mistress said something else. And only Ginger Bob, who was wise, as cats are, and who loved this tart old woman, could have believed what he was hearing.

"Ginger Bob," Miss Lomax said wearily, "I'm getting old, though I'll not admit it to a soul except you. But I'm getting old. And I wish—I wish I could have a fresh start. But it's too late to think about things like that, isn't it? It's much too late!"

Briony's Garden

THE next day, Briony had a letter. This was an unusual occurrence, for letters for her were few and far between, except at Christmas, when she always had a fair number of cards and parcels, and on her birthday. Apart from that, there were very few occasions when her friends wrote to her, for if they did want to contact her, they usually found it quicker and cheaper to use the telephone.

So Briony did not rip open her letter at once, but carried it out to the garden, to savour it to the full, before she opened it. She put it down with a big stone to anchor it, although this was an unnecessary precaution, for the day was quite airless. And she worked doggedly for some time, resisting the impulse to open it, until the time had come for her elevenses. She went in to wash her hands, and found Mark on the same errand.

"Nice letter?" he asked kindly, passing the soap.

"I haven't opened it yet; I'm keeping it for my break," Briony said solemnly. "I get so few letters that I wanted to make the most of having one."

"My word! Wouldn't it be a pity if it was an invitation to something exciting this morning!" Mark teased, and Briony looked alarmed.

"Goodness, I hadn't thought of that! I hope it isn't. But surely they would have rung instead?"

Mark merely chuckled and looked provoking, and so it was with a racing heart that Briony took her little tray out into the garden. She sat down and opened the precious letter. It proved to be from Heather.

"Dear Briony," she read. "I expect you will be surprised to get a letter from me, but I am unexpectedly going to stay with my Aunt Jean for a few days. I got this from Pat yesterday and somehow I feel you ought to have it as soon as possible. I hope you like it and that God will use it to speak to you.

"How is the garden getting along? and how are you getting on with your Miss Lomax? I'll look forward to hearing all your news when I get back, but will ring you when I do.

"Love,

Heather."

"P.S. Isn't Jesus wonderful?"

Eagerly, Briony opened the thick, folded paper

which was inside the letter. She smoothed it out
and began to read.

The Gardener

My garden was like a wilderness
Where nothing grew.
Nothing was beautiful, nothing was useful.
The ground was parched and choked with weeds
And yet I felt no touch of shame
Till the Gardener came.

"You won't do any good with this one," I said.
"It's been left too long in that condition.
Nothing will grow there; everything's dead."
He smiled.
"I'm rather good at achieving the impossible.
May I try?" the Gardener said.

"You can have a go if you like," I said reluctantly.
"After all—I mean—it won't do any harm to try.
But it's a pretty hopeless proposition.
I can't even see where to start."
"Well, let's begin right at the heart," He said.
And smiled at me.
"Look! I'll show you how beautiful it *could* be."

I was beginning to feel interested, in spite of myself.
So I watched as He drew a plan of my garden,
And explained the rules for keeping it neat.

It did look nice, His plan of it,
And I wished it really looked like that.
"Would you like it? You can have it, you know.
The work will be hard and the progress slow."
"I couldn't remember the rules, I don't think."
"Oh, don't worry," He said. "They're already in
   print."

I looked at the garden and then at His eyes
And I suddenly wanted to squirm inside.
"It—wasn't always this bad, you know.
But the weeds get in—and then—they just grow."
The Gardener looked and then gently said "Yes,
I see what you mean; it *is* rather a mess."

And yet it was *my* garden. Why should I care
About His opinion of it? It was mine.
True, He had given it to me, but—
"I'm not very good at it I'm afraid," I said.

Take it or leave it, I thought.
I was tired of making excuses for my garden.
These things happen to the best of us
And yet——

"May I take over?" the Gardener said.
"It is my job, and you must admit
That you made rather a mess of it."

So I said
"Yes. Come in and take over, please."
And He came
Into my garden in all its shame.

He began the work and then I joined Him,
But there was nothing I could do to help.
I tried, but it was impossible.
And as He rooted out the weeds and dragged the
    choking briars away,
I saw how His hands, feet, even His head
Were torn by them, and the wounds bleeding.
And I said
"Did you do this for me? I didn't know
That it would cause you to suffer so!"

At last, the garden was cleared; the weeds were
    taken away,
And the garden was ready for planting, with seeds
    which were there to stay.
For the Gardener knew all my weakness; He knew
    which seeds He had sown.
And He promised, the day that I asked Him in,
    that I would never be left alone.
So He planted the seeds of Faith and Hope,
    Repentance, Humility, Peace,
And He gave me the bird Joy to sing there the
    songs that will never cease.
And now, as I work there for love of Him and am
    endlessly weeding there,

I cherish the seeds which He loves best, that my
garden be not bare.

For when the lease is eternally up, and He comes
to my garden to stay,

I should like to have a show of flowers to give Him,
on that Day.

Briony put the paper down, and her lips were
trembling.

"My garden," she whispered. "My garden."

She looked at the chaos in front of her. Some
digging had been done, but even there, the weeds
were defiantly pushing through again. And there
was so much work remaining. She knew very well
that weeds grew more quickly than flowers, and
how difficult it was to get them out when you
wanted to. And as she looked into her life, she
could see the same principle applied.

Bad habits became ingrained and it was difficult
to break them—and yet so easy to say "It's my
life and I can do what I like with it." She could
say that about her garden. But how much more
sensible to take the advice of people who knew
something about it! And, with her life, how much
better it would be if she gave it into the control of
the Gardener, who really owned the garden, and
had only rented it out for a short time.

Briony wanted to make a beautiful garden, and
she wanted people to admire it. Yet she realised

more each day that she knew very little about it.
She needed help with it; whether it was advice
from Miss Lomax, or the practical help which her
father gave by digging for her. And as the realisa-
tion grew on her, she looked again into her life.
And she looked at her garden.

And then, the things which she had heard from
the eager lips of Heather and Jessamy fell into
place. Bits of the Bible which she had read without fully understanding the implications, came
home with new and wonderful meaning. And
Briony found that Jesus Himself suddenly became
real to her. From being someone she had only
heard and read about, He suddenly became a
distinct and vivid personality. He became the
Friend Who would always be there; the Gardener
Who could root out the most obstinate and the
most deeply buried weeds. He became, as she, as
well as Heather, saw, the answer to the difficult
and sometimes frightening things which young
people couldn't understand. But most of all, He
was shown as the most amazing and wonderful
Love which she had ever known in her life. The
great and mighty God, Who had made all the
world, had hurled shining planets into space and
raised up the mighty mountains, cared about *her*,
Briony Hunter. He had known that she would not
be able to live as fully and happily as she ought in

her own strength. She would need Jesus to do it for her.

But God was holy and perfect and wonderful. How could Briony, with a sinful nature go to God, even if she wanted to? And of course, as Briony saw, she couldn't. God's holiness demanded satisfaction. So Jesus had lived a perfect life and then died that terrible death to bring Briony and everyone else in the world to Himself. His blood was the price that God demanded. Jesus was God. Only God could, for man, plead with God. So it was done.

Jesus is alive! thought Briony, in new wonder. Now she saw why Heather and Jessamy were so excited about it. It *was* exciting. It was wonderful and, to Briony, it was completely new. God loves me! she thought, almost dazed by the sudden wonder of it. God loves *me*!

She stood staring up at the trees for a moment. Then she looked back at the garden, and hesitantly, but with a wonderful confidence, she found herself speaking to Someone Who had suddenly become so precious.

"Dear Jesus, I just didn't realise before. But now I do. Please help me to understand more and more and to love you. I believe that you died on the cross to bring me to God. I believe that you won the victory on Calvary and that you are alive now. And I don't know why you should, but I believe you want to be my Friend, too. I think I might make an awful mess of my life, if I run it on my own. Please come into my life and look after it for me. I want you to come into my life more than I have ever wanted anything else before."

And so, of course, He came. As He had promised.

7

In a Caravan

ONCE her prayer had finished, Briony was not very sure what to do next. She opened her eyes as widely as she could and looked around her. Everything was just the same. It was another scorching hot day and the sky was a deep, vivid blue, with not a cloud to be seen. The grass and trees were brilliantly green, and there were bright splashes of colour all over the garden, where flowers defied "the jungle" to keep them down. The birds were singing joyously and Briony suddenly wanted to join in. So she jumped up in the air as high as she could and shouted:

"Yippee!" at the top of her voice.

Mark, who was wandering round the garden in a desultory kind of way noticed her, and went over to join her before she had noticed *him*. When she did, she stood stock still and felt supremely silly.

"Hallo! Doing a war dance?" he asked with interest.

"No," Briony mumbled, hoping he would go away. But Mark was filling in time before dinner, and was inclined, as most brothers are, to tease. So he tried again.

"Bitten by an ant?"

"No," Briony said crossly. Why, oh why, did Mark have to choose that particular time to be in the garden, when he usually avoided it like the plague, in case he was asked to do any work? Mark tried yet again:

"It must be a touch of the sun. Let big brother feel——" and he stretched out to feel Briony's forehead. She retaliated with a shove and they grappled together for a few minutes. Finally she flung away.

"Go *away*, Mark! Who asked you to come and interfere?"

"I didn't know that I was interfering, but I certainly won't go on," Mark said, irritated. "I certainly don't want to be with Miss Crosspatch!"

And whistling under his breath, he strolled towards the house, leaving Briony flushed and angry and nearly in tears. Oh, what a dreadful thing to happen! *And* at the worst possible moment! How *could* she be so cross with Mark? He hadn't meant any harm, and after all, he had worked hard on two very hot afternoons to help her with her garden. Briony's lips trembled, but she picked up her fork and went resolutely on with her weeding.

While Mark, feeling decidedly aggrieved, went into the house.

"What's eating Briony?" he demanded of his mother, whom he found preparing dinner.

"With Briony? Nothing that I know of. In fact, she's been very chirpy lately, what with her garden and these new friends, and exploring the countryside and so on. Why?"

"Well, she just bit my head off for no reason at all," Mark complained.

His mother looked up in surprise.

"Did she? That's not like Bri. Maybe she's overdoing her gardening and getting tired. I'll try to persuade her to go out this afternoon. Or you could take her with you."

"Thank you for nothing," Mark said sourly. "As I said to her just now, *I* don't want to be with Miss Crosspatch."

"She isn't usually a crosspatch. *Something* must have upset her," Mrs. Hunter said, rather perturbed; and when Briony came in, she tackled her.

"You look hot and bothered, Bri. Is anything the matter?"

"No," Briony said quickly.

Her mother gave her a sharp look.

"Sure? You look as though things are getting a bit on top of you."

"Well, they aren't. I've never been happier in my life," Briony said defiantly.

"That's good, then. But I think you have done enough in the garden for a bit. Take this afternoon off. You could go into Nether Walden and see your friends."

"Heather's gone away to her auntie for a few days," Briony said, but her eyes brightened. After all, she could always go and see Jessamy. She looked wistfully at Mark when he came in, but he ignored her.

"Mark?" she said tentatively.

"What is it, crosspatch?"

"Don't call me that," Briony said, with the suspicion of a quiver in her voice. "I'm—I'm sorry I *was* a crosspatch; that's all."

"O.K." said Mark, and they all went into dinner together peacefully enough. But afterwards, Briony made haste to get ready to go out. Jessamy was a bit quick-tempered, and inclined to be a bit bossy at times, but she would, Briony felt, understand these strange new feelings of hers. And she would *certainly* understand about saying sharp things without meaning to. So it was with hope in her heart that Briony boarded the bus to Nether Walden.

It was a great disappointment to find no one at home, and Briony nearly gave up and went

straight back. But she decided to fill in a little
time by going to the gospel stall in the market and
looking round. Mr. Jephson, who owned the
stall, knew her now, and so did the pretty, fair
girl, who had said her name was Carol. As Briony
approached the stall, she could see, deep in con-
versation with another girl, Carol herself. The
other girl was about Carol's age, or maybe a little
older. Her long dark hair was coiled up at the
back of her neck; she had on a pale blue cotton
dress and looked delightfully fresh and cool. Both
girls smiled as they saw Briony approaching and
Carol said:

"Hullo, Briony. On your own today?"

Before Briony could answer, the girl in blue
turned to her, and gave her a searching look.
Then she said:

"I've been wanting to meet you, if you are who
I think you are. And it isn't a very common
name, so I think you *are* who I think you are.
You *are* Heather and Jessamy's Briony, aren't
you?"

"Yes," Briony admitted, though she looked
rather startled, as well she might. "But you—oh!
Are you by any chance—are you *possibly* Heather
and Jessamy's Pat?"

They all laughed.

"Pat I am," the girl in blue agreed. "I'm very

pleased to meet you, Briony. I've heard a lot about you lately. You are the girl who loves gardens?"

"Yes, and you're the one that the poem 'The Gardener' belongs to," Briony said promptly. "Did you write it?"

Pat laughed again.

"No; I can't write poems. It was written by a friend of mine, Briony. So Heather has already sent it to you? Did you like it?"

"Yes, very much." Briony hesitated and then said shyly, "I was coming to talk to Jessamy, because of something which happened because of it, but she isn't in, either, and I don't quite know what to do now."

"Oh?" Pat gave her a quick look. "Could *I* be of any help?"

"Would you?" Briony asked, still shyly. "I really do want to talk to someone—and no one at home is any use with things like this."

Carol had been listening quietly, watching the pair of them with quick eyes. Now she intervened.

"I was just deciding that it was time and more that I had my tea break. Mr. Jephson has had his. Why don't you come and have a cup of tea with me? And then you can borrow the caravan and have your talk in peace, if Briony wants to talk. Markets are all very well, but they aren't always the best place to have a peaceful talk about the Lord Jesus—if that was what you *did* want to talk about."

"Yes, it was, actually," Briony said, reddening. "How did you guess?"

Carol gave her a very warm smile.

"I didn't guess, but I thought it was quite likely. After all, Heather and Jessamy have talked to *us* about their Briony, too, and we have all been praying for you."

Briony was nearly overcome.

"Praying for me? But how lovely of you!"

"Not a bit. We were pleased to do it."

Carol looked round the side of the stall and caught Mr. Jephson's eye.

"All right if I go for my tea break now? And Pat and Briony would like to borrow the van for a chat, if it is free?"

"It's always free for the Lord's work, Carol; you know that," was the quick rejoinder. "God bless you!"

"I knew he would agree like a shot," Carol confided, leading the way to a large blue caravan near by. "But it's only polite to ask. Come in, both of you," and she unlocked the door of the blue van and held it hospitably open.

Briony had never been in a caravan before, and

she looked around her with interest. But the first thing she noticed was that it seemed more like an office than an ordinary caravan. True, there was a comfortable-looking bunk bed along one wall and a coloured flap had been lifted to show a tiny sink underneath. Next to it there was an equally tiny cooker, and two or three cupboards. And there was a table on which a vase of bright flowers reposed, and tuck-away chairs round it, and fitted cupboards which could obviously be used for books, or clothes, or anything you liked. All that was quite ordinary. It was the rest which wasn't.

Briony spent several fascinated minutes browsing through all the things for sale, while Carol brewed tea and Pat, who had evidently visited the van before, fished for biscuits and buns, and they made quite a merry party. But all too soon Carol said that she must get back to the stall.

"Stay here as long as you want to," she said to Pat. "I'll leave you the key. When you've finished, just drop it back to one of us, will you? You know the time we pack up, but I don't suppose you will be as long as that. Not that it matters if you are."

She smiled at them both, and quietly left the van, leaving Briony feeling most dreadfully shy and rather awkward, not knowing what to say or do. There was a pause and then Pat said calmly:

"Now you're feeling absolutely terrible, aren't you?"

Briony was about to deny this, but she looked up and caught Pat's eye. She looked at her doubtfully for a minute. Then she giggled, unexpectedly. Pat laughed.

"That's better! Don't worry, Briony. I can imagine how you feel. It would be strange if you *didn't* feel shy and a bit awkward and nervous. After all, you hardly know me."

"I've heard quite a lot about you, though," Briony said, taking heart from this understanding attitude. "And I really *do* need someone to talk to. I knew Heather was away, but I hadn't reckoned on Jessamy being out, too. So if you really don't mind——?"

"You know I don't." Pat got up from the table and began to clear the cups away. "I'll just wash these up for Carol and then we'll have a good chat. But fire away now, if you want to."

Somehow, it was easier to begin when Pat wasn't looking at her. So Briony took a deep breath and said:

"It's all been a bit *sudden*—and I'm bewildered. You see, until I came here and met Heather and Jessamy, I hadn't really thought of God at all. He was just someone who was occasionally mentioned at school—but I never thought that He could have any connection with me. And more than that, I'd never imagined that He could *want* to have anything to do with me. I mean, I always thought that I was here—and God was up there— and it didn't seem that we would ever be in a position to meet, though as I said, I hadn't thought much about it."

Briony paused; trying to arrange her muddled thoughts. Pat wiped the cups, put them safely away into one of the little cupboards, hung up the cloth and then sat down. Briony looked at her doubtfully, and then went on, rather uncertainly:

"And then—just by chance—I met Heather and Jessamy. It was here, in the market, and they came across and told me that Jesus is alive—and we went on from there. And I could see that it wasn't just words—that it really did mean something to them, because they were so excited about it. And yet they weren't all gooey and superior, if you see what I mean?"

Pat smiled, but she saw that Briony was looking at her rather anxiously, so she said:

"Yes, Briony, I do know what you mean. And you know, it wasn't chance that you all met. There is no such thing as chance in the lives of the children of God. I am sure that there was a loving hand guiding all three of you to the time that Heather and Jessamy came up to you and told that they knew Jesus was alive, and they wanted to share it with you. And I'm sure you were right that they were genuinely excited about it. I think that is a very common reaction when someone realises that the great God of Heaven has come to earth for *them*."

"Yes, that's how I felt this morning. But then it went all wrong," Briony said helplessly, and Pat looked at her with new interest.

"Can you tell me a bit more about it, Briony? *How* did you feel this morning?"

"Well, you see, ever since Heather and Jessamy told me about Jesus and all that, it seemed important to me, even though I didn't understand it —and still don't really. Then, when I was working in my garden, it suddenly made sense, and I could see that wrong things in someone's life could spoil it, just like weeds can choke and kill in a garden. And I could see that what Heather and Jessamy said was true, and that Jesus wanted to be my Friend. So I asked Him to."

She stopped and looked shyly at Pat.

"That's splendid!" Pat said warmly. "No wonder you wanted to come and tell Jessamy about it! I'm so very glad, Briony. But there's more, isn't there?"

"Yes. You see," Briony said confidentially, "I did ask Jesus to come and be my Friend and I believe that He did come. But it made me feel that I wanted to shout and sing and dance, so I capered about in the garden—and—and then Mark came over and started teasing me. And I couldn't tell him why I felt so excited, and he kept on, and I got cross, and then I felt that I'd let Jesus down good and proper, and I wondered—I wondered——"

". . . if it was really true after all?" finished Pat, and Briony gulped and nodded.

"How did you know?"

"Because you're human, my dear. Because everyone who commits their life to Jesus wants to make it a good life to offer Him. And because the devil tempts *everyone* by letting something like that happen, and then taking advantage of it by making us doubt that Jesus is really with us. But it *is* only temptation and it *is* only doubt. Jesus can be trusted, Briony; He really can. And if He said He would come to you as your Friend and Saviour and you have asked Him to, you can be sure that He has done just that, *whatever* the devil tells you and however loudly he shouts."

"That's a relief," Briony said frankly.

"It's a definite thing, though. Is Mark your brother?"

"Yes. He's older than me: fourteen. And he *always* teases; I don't usually mind so much, but . . ."

". . . you were in rather a whirl," Pat finished sympathetically. "But you told him you were sorry?"

"Oh yes."

"And did he accept it?"

"Yes, I think so."

"And did you tell Jesus you were sorry to let Him down?"

Briony wriggled uncomfortably.

"Well, no. I wasn't sure that I could go to Him just like that. I didn't feel He would be very pleased to see me."

"Do you mind your mother seeing you when you are grubby in the garden?" Pat asked, and Briony stared in surprise.

"Of course not! She's my mother!"

"And God is your Father," said Pat quietly. "Never forget that, Briony. Now you belong to Jesus, Heaven is your real home and Heaven means, quite simply, the presence of God. And you are never too grubby to go to Him, because Jesus has promised to cleanse you."

Briony gave a sigh of relief.

"So that's all right! What shall I do about Mark?"

"Don't force anything," Pat said calmly. "Just wait until it seems that there is a suitable moment —and that goes for telling all your family."

"I thought I ought to," Briony acknowledged. "And I shall feel a bit silly, but I will."

"Now, Briony, about your garden."

"My garden?" Briony looked up in real surprise. "I thought we were talking about me and Jesus?"

"We are," Pat said, smiling. "And if that poem helped you, as you said early on that it did, then you will see what I mean by your garden."

Briony thought again, and reddened.

"Yes, of course. My life is the garden for Jesus to work in, isn't it?"

"That's right," Pat agreed. "But you can help Him. What do you need to make a garden? In ordinary terms, I mean?"

"Well, you need the garden itself," Briony said slowly. "Whether it's a gorgeous big park, or just a little window box—and you can do quite a lot with a window box. But you have to have *some* ground to work on.

"Then you need weather—wind and sun and rain—otherwise things won't grow. You need plants, and you have to know whether they like shade or the sun, and lots of water or hardly any. And you have to keep at it; I mean, it's no good expecting even a window box to look after itself. You have to weed and water and so on. Is that the sort of thing you meant?"

"Yes," Pat agreed. "Now let's try and put all your very practical and sensible ideas into human terms. You already have your 'garden'—no need to worry about a window box! And God has chosen your particular family and the area where you live. The equivalent of rain and wind and sun to help a Christian grow is prayer, Bible study and meeting with other Christians. That includes public worship in church, as well. And although we can't work out our salvation ourselves, we can and must persevere. That means 'sticking at it' just as much as keeping a check on your garden."

"I've hardly ever read the Bible," Briony confessed, "and my family doesn't go to church. They will think it strange if I start to do both."

"I expect they will," Pat agreed, "but if you can do it and be natural about it, you will probably find that they not only accept that you want to do these things, but they might be interested enough to ask you why you are doing them. Then, if you tell them that you are doing these things because you love Jesus, that might start them thinking about Jesus for themselves."

"That would be terrific," Briony agreed,

beaming. "But which bit of the Bible should I read first?"

"If you like—and this is only an idea—I'll let you have a set of the study notes which Heather and Jessamy use. You might find them helpful; they are prepared for people of your sort of age. I think there are some here, so hold on, and I'll look them out."

Later, Briony positively skipped off to catch her bus, feeling thoroughly reassured. Indeed, she felt so happy that it was a shock to encounter a woebegone Sarah at the garden gate.

"What's the matter, poppet?"

"Simon won't play with me," said Sarah sorrowfully. "He's playing football with Mark, and he says dolls are silly. Will *you* play dolls?"

She looked at her sister so hopefully that Briony hadn't the heart to say no. They were just making their way to the house when there was a whoop and Simon dashed towards them.

"Bri? Come and play football? I can't beat Mark."

"I've said I'll play dolls with Sarah," Briony began, and Simon groaned.

"Dolls! What's the good of dolls? Football's the thing. Up with the team, three cheers for the

goal-keeper and down with the ref! **Come on,
Bri!**"

"Well——" Briony thought hastily. "I'll **tell**
you what. You go and practise shooting goals,
and Sarah and me'll dress the dolls. Then we can
bring them to the match and they can be spectators. You can't have a proper match without
spectators, you know. You need someone to
cheer! Will that do?"

"That'll do. Don't be too long, though. **Down**
with the ref!" and Simon whooped off into the
garden again, leaving his sisters looking at each
other.

"It isn't even the football season," Briony said,
but Sarah shook her head.

"Simon says *any* time's a good time to play football. Can I borrow your stripey scarf for Teddy?"

"You shall," Briony promised, and they went
off hand in hand.

An Addition to the Family

TO Briony's great disappointment, she was not able to go round to see Miss Lomax as quickly as she would have liked. Her announcement that she wanted to go to church on Sunday morning aroused little comment from her family, apart from a warning not to be late, as they were all going out that afternoon.

Briony enjoyed the service, and meeting Jessamy's young brother, Bruce, and her heart was warmed by Jessamy's rapturous reception of the news that Briony, too, was trusting in Jesus. She and Pat introduced her to several of their friends, including a Mrs. Denison, who was the leader of the girls' Bible Class, and she received a warm invitation to join them when the classes started again in September. So Briony felt very happy as she joined her family in the car after dinner, and tried to coax her father to tell her where they were going. But although he threw out the most maddening and frequent hints, he refused to disclose their actual destination.

"Do *you* know where we are going, Mother?"

Briony asked, as they left the village behind them.

Mrs. Hunter laughed.

"Yes, of course I know. Dad and I decided some time ago that today would be quite suitable for this—er—excursion."

"I don't suppose it's anything really exciting," Mark said.

Mr. Hunter smiled at his wife and said lightly:

"You never know. Just for once, you might get as excited as the younger ones."

"I doubt it," Mark said coolly. "I don't go in for whoopings and shriekings like the kids."

"Oh, not everyone reacts in the same way. And it's not so many years since you whooped and shrieked with the best of them," Mrs. Hunter reminded him.

The twins crowed in unison. They loved their elder brother when he condescended to play with them or take them out, but at fourteen, Mark was beginning to feel that this was very much beneath his dignity, and in consequence, the twins often found him as aggravating as Briony did.

"Mark's a superior ass," Simon began: but Mr. Hunter intervened firmly, "Now don't start calling each other names. It will only lead to a fight, and we want this to be a pleasant family outing."

Even the twins usually obeyed at once when

their father spoke in that tone, and Briony was
certainly not going to say anything which might
provoke her brother again. She turned to her
father.

"Dad! How far away is—wherever we're
going?"

"Oh, only another ten miles or so. It won't
take us long," Mr. Hunter said. "How did you
get on this morning, Bri? Enjoy yourself?"

"Mm. Heather is still away, but Pat and
Jessamy were there—and Jessamy's little brother.
It was a nice service," Briony said tentatively.
"Can I go regularly?"

"Yes, unless we are going off for the day. We
could hardly leave you all alone," Mr. Hunter
said. "End House is a bit more isolated than
where we were living before, you know."

"I could go to Pat—or Heather—or——" began Briony, but her mother shook her head.

"We will talk it over later. It isn't fair to your
father to try and sort out problems when he is
driving along a strange road. Besides, I thought
you enjoyed our week-end outings?"

"Oh, I do," Briony said. "Only—well, I'm
older now. And there are other things——"

She stopped, floundering. But help came from
a most unexpected quarter.

"You know," Mark said, "I rather agree with

Briony. It's all right going off together and all that, but Bri's right. We *are* getting older. I expect there will be lots of times when *I* shan't want to come, either. So I could keep an eye on the kid."

Briony was so pleased at this unexpected support that she quite forgave him for calling her "the kid" although it usually made her indignant. Mr. Hunter regarded his two eldest with amusement.

"You are a funny pair! Your mother and I were afraid that you would be bored stiff in the country, after the busy life you had on the estate. And even there you used to wail that you didn't know what to do on a Sunday, unless we went out! Still, we'll leave it there for the time being. Turn round, Mark. You are missing all the scenery."

Mark, surprised, looked round. Then he gave a shout.

"Aubrey Kennels! I say, Dad! Are we going to buy a *dog*?"

"We are. At least," said Mr. Hunter prudently, "we are going to look at some puppies. There are several litters for sale here, and we always meant to have a dog as soon as we had enough space to let the poor creature move around. Besides, as I said a few minutes ago, End

House is a bit isolated. I want a dog which will not only be game for a romp, but will also guard the house." He looked at Mark and smiled. "Excited after all?"

"You bet! I didn't think of a *dog*," Mark said, and he smiled back at his father and his eyes glowed. A dog had been a dream of his for years, but it had always seemed that it would be a dream which would not be fulfilled. His parents, who had been brought up with animals, had sympathised, but had held out that their previous home had been unsuitable for dogs. But when they knew that they were moving to End House, almost the first thing which Mrs. Hunter had said to her husband was:

"Now Mark can have his dog," and Mr. Hunter had agreed.

"Just one thing," Mr. Hunter said. "This is a *family* dog. We all help; we all enjoy him. So no arguments. O.K.?"

"O.K.," the family agreed in chorus.

"Then out you get," Mr. Hunter said briskly, and they all scrambled out eagerly.

"I hear doggy noises," Sarah announced, taking her mother's hand. "Will they be friendly dogs?"

"Of course. You're surely not frightened?" Mrs. Hunter asked.

"No-o," Sarah said, rather doubtfully, and her father smiled.

"If any child of mine is afraid of dogs, then it *is* time we had one!"

"*I'm* not 'fraid," Simon said stoutly. "But dogs bite."

"Only usually to defend themselves. Most dogs are friendly to humans unless they have been cruelly treated," Mr. Hunter said, firmly. "Now let's go and find Mr. Aubrey. I told him on the phone that we would arrive about this time."

They walked up the wide drive, round the corner, and found themselves at the kennels. They could see, at the end of the very extensive grounds, a row of small wooden houses and a few pens. Dogs were running about, dogs were in pens, and all over came the noises of dogs talking. And Mr. Aubrey, kind, tall and with twinkling brown eyes, soon appeared, to welcome them, and to explain that they were to take all the time they wanted to look around.

"You can choose your dog," he ended, "but your dog can't choose *you*! And we love our dogs and want them all to go to homes where they will really be a loved member of the family. So be very sure."

That was the beginning of a delightful afternoon, and it continued with them being introduced to the family dogs—Mipsy, the little old Yorkshire terrier——

". . . who is the smallest, but also the oldest, and knows she is boss. All the others are very firmly under her paw, and she doesn't stand any nonsense from any puppy, no matter how big and boisterous."

Then there was Peter, a black labrador; Anna, the blind golden cocker; a dachshund called Humphrey, who was Mrs. Aubrey's special pet; and a young golden retriever called Rory.

Rory greeted them very effusively, and Mr. Aubrey kept a watchful eye on Sarah, who looked doubtful. Then, as they went on their way, they were joined by a young man in jeans, who was accompanied by a beautiful red setter, who capered to meet them on springing, feathery legs.

"And this," said Mr. Aubrey, gently pushing her away from Sarah, who had shrunk back, "is my son Adrian and his dog Conkers."

"She's *beautiful*," Briony said fervently.

"She needs to be. She hasn't any brains," Mr. Aubrey said frankly, and there was an indignant snort from his son.

"She's a rattling good mother, and she has beautiful pups."

"Early days. She's had *one* good litter," Mr.

Aubrey amended, and grinned after his son's departing figure.

"Adrian adores her and won't hear a word against her, but even he admits that she hasn't much sense. In fact, I happen to know that he privately calls her 'Bonkers' instead of 'Conkers'. Now, come this way, will you? There is something which I want this young lady to see."

He took Sarah's hand, and led her off, the others following. "Something" proved to be a litter of black and golden labradors, only six weeks old, who were curled up together, asleep in a warm, soft heap. Briony was enraptured, and Mr. Aubrey smiled at Sarah's face. One of the puppies quivered and woke, and he lifted it gently out from the others and placed it in Sarah's willing arms.

"Now, you aren't going to be frightened of that little baby thing, are you? That's right"—as Sarah cuddled the warm puppy—"you make friends."

After that, Sarah lost the last of her fears, and willingly petted all the dogs they saw, including some lively young retrievers. This breed was very popular with them all, although Briony had a soft spot for the beautiful Conkers and would have liked a setter puppy. Mr. Aubrey, true to his word, did nothing to hurry them, and was very willing for them to meet the mothers of the various puppies, and Mark fell in love with one; a beautiful golden retriever of four years old, who had five puppies.

"I like her best," he said decidedly.

"I don't," said Briony, who was cuddling two puppies at once: marvelling at the softness of their coats, and tickling their bare pink tummies, while they snuffled at her with inquisitive noses, and chewed her fingers with their tiny needle-sharp teeth.

"We *must* have a puppy; a little one," Simon begged. He and Sarah were playing with the other three, and looked as though they would need steel chains to tear them away!

"I'm sorry, Mark," Mr. Aubrey said—he had long since learned all their names—"but the mother isn't for sale. Only the puppies. Come and see some more."

He led them firmly away to another pen.

"Just like a tiny garden," Briony said, and her mother smiled.

"A puppy garden, I think. Oh, look. Airedales!"

"Mum! Just like your Nell!" Mark shouted at the same time.

"I had an Airedale called Nell," Mrs. Hunter

told Mr. Aubrey. "And she was so lovely, and such a good guard, too. And——"

"Come in and see them," Mr. Aubrey invited. They went into the pen and three lovely Airedale puppies gambolled to meet them. A bitch followed them.

"Their mother still spends some time with them. Come here, puppies," Mr. Aubrey said invitingly, and the three bounced over to him; eagerly licking his hand, pulling at his shoe-laces and generally enjoying themselves. And then one suddenly turned and went straight to Mrs. Hunter. It licked her hand, looked at her expectantly, and then gave a little bark.

"What did the puppy say?" asked Sarah.

"I *think* it said it would like us for its family," Mrs. Hunter said, smiling. She picked the puppy up. "I don't think she is quite old enough to leave her mother. But is she sold already?"

Briony is Anxious

ONE of the puppies was already sold. Out of the other two, one was a dog, and Mrs. Hunter wanted a bitch, so it was the puppy which had gone to her which they bought.

". . . as if she *knew* she belonged to us," Briony said admiringly. It was strange how suddenly they had all decided on the Airedale puppy, but it was so, and they had a happy, noisy drive back, discussing the fun they would have with their puppy. They would be able to fetch her in another week, as she would be eight weeks old by then, and that was considered the right age to leave her mother.

But when the twins, wildly excited, had gone to bed, Mr. Hunter said:

"There is something which I don't know if you realise, Bri, but that is that a puppy—and a young dog, for that matter—is death and ruin to a garden. Would you rather leave your rockery for another year or two?"

"Oh no," Briony said, dismayed. "I want to start."

"So you shall, then. I'll get some strong wire netting and fence it around, if need be," her father promised. "After all, it won't be too soon for her to learn that there are places where she mustn't go. Now, you two. What is all this about weekend outings? Why don't you want to come?"

It was Briony's chance. And she gulped hard, but she took it.

"Because I want to go to church with my friends. And I want to do that because I want to learn more about Jesus. Just yesterday I realised that Jesus was alive and wanted me for a friend, and it's so wonderful!"

"Is *that* why you were capering round the garden like a mad thing?" Mark asked accusingly.

Briony blushed.

"Yes, it was. It was all so new and exciting and I was thrilled. I *am* sorry I snapped at you."

"Well, I don't understand quite what you mean, but I am glad you are pleased," Mr. Hunter said. "And how about inviting these friends of yours over for tea or something? You have been to them several times and the house is probably as decent now as it ever will be!"

"I hope we will improve on it a bit," Mrs.

Hunter murmured. "But I agree that it is time
we met your friends."

"I promised I'd ring up about next Sunday.
Can they come on Saturday?"

"Make it after Sunday and then they'll see the
puppy," Mark suggested and was rewarded by a
beaming smile from Briony.

"You're a super brother sometimes, Mark!"

"Thank you for nothing!" Mark grunted. But
he looked pleased.

"Now then, Mark!" Mr. Hunter swung round
on him. "What about the weekends?"

"I only said it wasn't up to much, going round
in a family gang all the time," Mark protested.
"Besides, we had piles of prep at our last school,
and I don't suppose this one will be better. It's
surely reasonable to want time for my own in-
terests."

"Quite reasonable," Mrs. Hunter agreed.
"And, if need be, you could give an eye to
Briony?"

"Yes, I suppose so. Though I draw the line at
taking her home if she's with a gang of girls."

"If I was, you needn't," Briony said smartly.
"And it won't be dark at Bible Class time. It will
only be church at night."

But Mrs. Hunter drew the line at this.

"Two churchy things in one day is quite

enough, and you said you wanted to try this
Bible Class. If you will both look after each other
and promise to be sensible, we shan't mind leaving you behind. Though when we go to visit
grandparents, you will come, of course."

Both Briony and Mark protested loudly at this.

"Must I?"

"Every time?"

"It's the twins everyone wants to coo over, not
a lad my age!"

"You're both being very silly," Mr. Hunter
said equably. "You know perfectly well that
your grandparents love you all. So that's
settled."

Settled it was, and as Briony washed, she began
to giggle. Why did nothing ever turn out as she
expected? She had vaguely thought that when
she told her family, they would react strongly:
either she would immediately be so wonderfully
changed by her trust in Jesus that her family
would follow her lead with tears of joy (instead of
which, she had had a fight with her brother!) or
they would oppose her violently and prevent her
from going to church—something which had happened in one of the books which Jessamy had lent
her!

What was it Miss Lomax had said? The reality
is more satisfying than the dream? For, when you

came to think of it, the reality was almost an anti-
climax. Oh, well! Briony grinned ruefully at her
reflection in the bathroom mirror. Come to think
of it, she didn't look the part of a martyr. It
would take Jessamy with her vivid dark looks, or
Heather with her cloud of golden hair and her
pink and white face. Not Briony Hunter, with her
cheerful grin, wild brown hair and the sort of
figure which had earned her the nickname of
"Chubs" at her last school.

She giggled again as she left the bathroom and
her mother, who was in the hall, heard her and
wanted to know the joke.

"Me, really," Briony said. "I was expecting all
sorts of fantastic things to happen when I told
you my news. And it's all been quite ordinary."

"Whatever did you expect?" Mrs. Hunter
asked in astonishment.

"That I might have to be a martyr," Briony
admitted, and her mother looked at her and
shouted with laughter.

"Bri, darling, anyone who looks less like a
martyr than you do, I should like to meet. Don't
be so silly! You know that your father and I don't
stand over you like warders. All we ask is that
you don't behave stupidly, make a nuisance of
yourself to other people, and do things you know

quite well to be dangerous. Now, please go and
finish washing, or the cocoa will be cold. Dad's
just made it."

"I *have* finished washing," Briony objected.

"Then try again," her mother said firmly. "I
can see a doggy paw-print up your arm. Get *that*
off, at least."

"You said 'wash your face and *hands*': you
didn't say anything about *arms*," the would-be
martyr grumbled, but she obediently went back
to the bathroom, leaving her mother, chuckling,
to go and break the news of Briony's thwarted
martyrdom to her husband, who enjoyed the joke
hugely.

The next day saw Briony concentrating on the
garden in the morning, and early in the afternoon
Mrs. Hunter took all the children for a bus-ride
into Maryton Vale, their nearest big town, to buy
Briony and Mark's school outfits. Both grumbled
and fidgeted, but were slightly cheered by ice-
cream sodas in a café, and then Mark thankfully
went home, taking the more cumbersome of the
parcels with him. He had got tea ready by the
time the others returned, which was a welcome
surprise. Tea over, Briony set off for Cypress
House. There was no sign of Miss Lomax in the
garden, but when she rang the bell, there was no
answer.

Briony was disappointed. She had been longing to share the news of this wonderful new Friend
with the lonely old lady, and it seemed that one
thing after another was preventing her from doing
so. Greatly daring, she went round to the greenhouse and peeped in. There was no one there.

"No good?" Mrs. Hunter asked, when she returned so quickly.

"No. No one seemed to be in. I hope she is all
right," Briony said uneasily.

"Why shouldn't she be all right?" Mark asked
impatiently.

Mrs. Hunter smiled.

"Don't start imagining wild things, Bri. After
all, I expect even Miss Lomax likes a walk on a
nice evening. She will be there tomorrow."

But she wasn't. In the morning, much to her
consternation, Briony again could get no answer.
Puzzled, disappointed, and still a little worried,
she waited round for a few moments and then
went home. But the uneasiness stayed with her
all day, and she could not shake it off. And, at
tea-time, she consulted her family, who wanted to
go out.

"There still isn't any answer from Miss Lomax
and I'm worried. Can you go without me? Then
I'll go round there."

"I suppose so," Mrs. Hunter said, rather doubtfully. Truth to tell, she had begun to wonder if the old lady had tired of Briony's visits and was deliberately not opening her door. But if this was so, perhaps it would be better for Briony to find out herself.

"All right. But be careful of the road if you're going on your bike, and don't stay too long. This hot weather must be very tiring for an old lady. We shan't be late, because of the twins' bedtime."

"I'll be *very* careful on the road," Briony promised, "and although I've lots to talk about, I won't stay long if you think better not. I can always go again another day. I won't be longer than about half an hour."

But she was. She was *much* longer than that!

What Happened That Night

BRIONY set off for Cypress House as fast as she dared, but taking care, as she had promised. Maybe she was being silly and fussy, but she felt that she would rather be sure. Miss Lomax had seemed so terribly alone in the world. It *was* possible that something could have happened to her and no one would either know or care.

No one answered the bell. So, greatly daring, she tried the front door. It was locked. So was the back one. She stood thinking, and jumped violently as something brushed against her legs. She looked down in a hurry.

"Ginger Bob!" she exclaimed, bending down to stroke the big cat. "So *you're* all right, at any rate. But where is your mistress?"

Ginger Bob rubbed against Briony and purred. Then he sat beside her and began to mew anxiously.

"I'm sorry, Ginger Bob," Briony said sadly. "I just don't understand cat language. Is Miss Lomax in bed?"

This was certainly a possibility. But if she was not, then she ought, by the law of averages, to be working in her garden. Or the greenhouse. Briony knew that Miss Lomax spent part of every day watering her precious seedlings in the greenhouse. There were always traces of moisture in the box and the plants looked strong. But now, as Briony realised, they did not. In fact, to be accurate, they were wilting. As they had been the night before. Which left Briony in no doubt that something was wrong.

"Oh," Briony thought, her head spinning. "What on earth shall I do?"

What she *should* have done, as she was afterwards told with some severity, was to find some responsible adult, preferably her own father or mother, to help her. But remembering how they had laughed off her ideas that something might be wrong, she was very reluctant to do this. What she actually did was to rush across the road to the public telephone, where she frantically dialled a number.

"Can I speak to Heather, please?—Heather, it's Briony . . . yes. Yes, it is super, but I didn't ring you up about that. Yes . . . there is something wrong. I need your help badly. No. Oh Heather, please don't ask questions, there isn't time. Can you come over on your bike right away —and bring Jessamy if you can? Oh, and will you bring a screwdriver?"

"A *what*?" gasped Heather at the other end.

"A screwdriver—a biggish one. And come to Cypress House in the village. Yes, it is. But please be quick!"

Heather and Jessamy were very quick, though it didn't seem like it to the anxious Briony. But in reality, it was only about fifteen minutes before they arrived, hot and breathless, and hurled themselves off their bicycles and on to their friend.

"Briony! What's all this?"

"Did you bring the screwdriver?"

"Yes. Two. What's up?" Jessamy asked simply, hauling a parcel from her saddlebag.

Briony told them in a few hurried sentences, and Jessamy was on to it in a flash.

"And you think something may have happened to her? Oh, I hope not! But why the screwdriver?"

"Because I want you to help me to break into the house," Briony said baldly, and they both gaped at her. Jessamy, as might have been expected, recovered first.

"Break into—Briony Hunter! Are you stark, staring, raving mad?"

"Not that I know of. Why?" Briony asked defiantly.

"Why? Because it's against the law, that's

why! We would get into fearful trouble. We might even be sent to prison."

"Rot!" Heather dismissed this. "We aren't old enough. People of twelve don't go to prison."

"Well, it would mean Borstal or something," Jessamy argued. "And that wouldn't be very nice, either."

Briony stamped her foot.

"Will you both stop jabbering and listen! All right, we may have to get into trouble. That's a risk I have to take. You needn't. But Miss Lomax is my friend, just as much as you two are. She's old and alone and she may be hurt. I don't care if there *is* a row. I'm going to get into that house and see for myself that nothing awful's happened. It's no good arguing. I've made up my mind."

The other two exchanged glances. Then Jessamy sighed and Heather looked resigned.

"All right. Where do we break in?"

"You mean you'll help?" Briony asked, and Jessamy sighed again.

"I still think you're raving mad, but you just might be right. And if you are, you will need help. Come on!"

"Right!" Briony led them round the back. "We couldn't open the doors, even if we knew how to pick locks. But there is a biggish window here and it's just fastened with screws; I know, because I've noticed it when I was in the house. I believe we could unscrew it and then I could crawl in, if you will bunk me up."

"Why not bunk *me* up? I'm the thinnest," Jessamy said maddeningly.

Briony glared at her, but refused to budge.

"I know you are, but that's neither here nor there. Miss Lomax doesn't know you and if she *is* all right, she'll be upset enough about people breaking in. A stranger would be even worse."

Jessamy accepted the sense of this, though with rather a bad grace, and they unwrapped the screwdrivers and began the somewhat tedious task of unfastening the window. It took a long time, for none of them were exactly expert with tools, and Briony became almost frantic as the minutes passed.

"Come *on*, Heather!"

"I'm being as quick as I can," Heather said, in a rather muffled voice. She had tucked her long fair hair under her chin in an effort to keep it out of the way. "But this isn't my usual occupation. Besides, neither of you is any better."

"It's coming now," Jessamy suddenly shouted. "Careful, Heather. It's shifting. You keep turning and we'll grab."

Heather turned and the other two grabbed and

a united shout of triumph went up as they moved the window open.

"Your Miss Lomax *can't* be around, or she would have heard all this row," Jessamy said. "Either that, or she's hurt. There, Briony. Can you get through there?"

"I *think* so," Briony said, regarding the space somewhat dubiously.

Fortunately, the window was of no great height, or in spite of all the shoving of her friends, Briony would not have got through. But she managed it, although she tore her blouse badly, and gave herself nasty cuts on her knees and head. A final shove from the others sent her right through, and she landed with a crash which caused her two friends to peer anxiously through the window and demand to know what had happened.

"I fell on a saucer. It's bust," Briony said dismally. Then she jumped back, as Ginger Bob leapt through the window. Making her way cautiously, she went to the back door, and drew back the bolts, with some difficulty, for they were both old and stiff. The other two rushed in.

"Ginger Bob!" Briony held out a pleading hand to the big cat. "Where is your mistress? Show us."

And Ginger Bob was only too pleased to do so.

Miaowing loudly, he led them to a small room which Miss Lomax obviously used as a sitting room. And there, at last, Briony found her. The three stopped short in horror.

"She isn't dead." Heather, who had done First Aid, had taken the cold hands in hers. "I can feel a pulse. But it's awfully weak. We ought to get a doctor at once."

"It's that nice Dr. Meadows, isn't it? I'll go and ring him up!" and Jessamy was away on the word. Heather went off in search of coats or rugs to place over the old lady, and Briony, left alone with her old friend, took one of the limp hands in hers.

"Please, Lord Jesus!" she begged silently. "Please don't let Miss Lomax die like this! Thinking that no one likes her or cares about her. Please don't let her die!"

Heather came back with a fine pile of rugs, and as they were laying them over the old lady, Briony suddenly stiffened. For Miss Lomax's eyelids had fluttered.

"Miss Lomax!"

There was a pause. Then Miss Lomax's eyes opened and she said weakly, "Briony—Hunter—is that really—you?"

"Yes, it's me. Are you all right?" Briony asked, blinking back tears of relief.

"I was—afraid——" The weak voice trailed off again, and the eyes closed. Then, with an obvious effort, she opened them again.

"—never any visitors—except you. And—I was—afraid that—you—would not come. Then —there would—be no one to care—for an old woman."

"There are plenty of people who will care, if you'll let them," Briony said stoutly. "I'm here and I care. My two friends are here, and they care, too. Most of all, the Lord Jesus cares. I wanted to tell you how much."

"I—used to know," the weak voice whispered. "But—so much—sorrow—I doubted——"

"You needn't," Briony assured her.

"Where is—Ginger Bob?"

"He's here. He's such a clever cat," Briony said eagerly. "It was Ginger Bob who showed us where you were. And he is quite all right."

"You—will—see that he—is looked after?"

"Yes, I promise. And shall I water the plants?"

A faint smile came over the white face.

"Yes, please—you—curious—child!"

It was her final effort. Miss Lomax lapsed into unconsciousness again, and this time she did not stir. But they had helped to move her into a more comfortable position while she was speaking and

then they had only a few seconds to wait before
Jessamy came panting in in the wake of Dr.
Meadows. Whatever he felt at the sight which
confronted him, all he said was:

"Bless my soul, quite a party! Now, what has
this obstinate old lady been and gone and done
now?"

He made a quick examination and then strode
to the telephone, and they could hear him order-
ing an ambulance, at which point, Briony's tears
returned. But he ordered her upstairs to find
nightie and washing things for Miss Lomax, so
that when she woke up in hospital she would find
some of her own things with her. Jessamy was
dispatched to find the village constable, for there
were valuable things in Cypress House. Heather
was instructed to feed Ginger Bob.

Thanks to the doctor's brisk efficiency, they
were all kept busy, but Briony felt very sad as she
saw her old friend going off alone in the ambulance. She had begged to go with her, but the
doctor refused to hear of it.

"Nonsense! Miss Lomax will wake up, have a
drink of milk or something, and settle down for a
long sleep. You look as though you could do with
one, too."

"Not yet," Briony said, sniffing, and wiping her
eyes with Heather's hanky—her own had given

out long ago. "I must water the plants. I promised."

The doctor looked at her, saw that she meant what she said, and gave in. "Right! But be as quick as you can. I'm going to telephone your father to come and fetch you. Heather, find me a bowl of water. Those cuts of Briony's need attention."

Heather went off meekly, and the doctor turned to the telephone again, and was soon speaking to a horrified Mr. Hunter.

"The old lady had had an accident and Bri found her? Oh *dear*. We knew she was worried, but I'm afraid—oh dear! She *will* be upset! And how did she get into the house?"

"I fancy we don't ask too many questions about that," the doctor said cheerfully. "But I'd be grateful if you could come and fetch her. She's had a bad shock."

"I'll be with you in fifteen minutes," Mr. Hunter said, and the line went dead.

He was as good as his word, and by the time he arrived, he found a pale, bandaged and tear-stained Briony waiting for him; at her feet a wicker basket which rocked as though whatever was in it did not care for its surroundings very much.

"Mr. Hunter? Dr. Meadows. Here is your

daughter, all ready for you. She's done a good job here, but she's all in now. Ginger Bob is in the basket. I *hope* he settles with you. The other two have gone home, and the police will look after the house. And as soon as I have seen you on your way, I am going to the hospital to see how Miss Lomax is, though I think she will be all right."

"You aren't just saying that?" Briony gulped, and he smiled at her.

"You're a brave girl, Briony, so I'll be honest with you. You know that bad falls aren't good for an old lady. And you know that being left to lie unconscious isn't good for her, either. But Miss Lomax is a wonderfully strong and determined old lady. She may have to stay in hospital for a few days, but I really do think she will be all right."

He had a few private words with Mr. Hunter and they parted. Mr. Hunter tied Briony's bike to the boot of the car, and they made all speed for home, where Mrs. Hunter was anxiously waiting.

"Is she all right? Have you got her safely?"

Briony leapt out of the car and ran to her mother as though she were no older than Sarah.

"Oh, Mother, I was right after all! And—and we broke into the house—and found her lying there—and—and I thought she was d-dead!"

"All right, Bri darling. Come in and tell us

about it. I don't quite understand what has happened, but I gather you have been very brave and sensible."

After Briony had told her story, she let Ginger Bob out of the cat basket and though he seemed restless and uneasy, he also seemed to realise that they were doing their best for him, and by the time Briony was safely in bed with a mug of cocoa, he seemed resigned to the fact that he had moved house. The sudden shrilling of the telephone startled them all.

"End House. Mr. Hunter speaking."

He ran upstairs a few moments later.

"That was Dr. Meadows, Bri. He thought you would like to know that Miss Lomax has come round, had a drink and settled to sleep. You can go to see her tomorrow. Good night, darling. Things will be much brighter in the morning."

A Good End to the Summer

THINGS *were* much brighter in the morning.
Briony, who slept till very late, had her breakfast in bed as a treat, and then rang up the hospital, where she was delighted to learn that Miss
Lomax had also slept well, and could be visited.
Then, after she had replaced the receiver, the
phone rang, and it proved to be Heather, who
gave a cry of joy when she heard her friend's
voice.

"Oh Briony! Are you all right? How's your
head and leg?"

"Oh—all right!" Briony casually dismissed her
noble wounds. "Mother's going to take off the
bandages and put on sticking plaster, so they
won't look so horrific when I go to see Miss Lomax
this afternoon. Would you like to come,
too?"

There was a pause, during which Briony could
hear Heather conferring with Jessamy, who, as
she had guessed, was there too. But in the end,
they decided that Briony should go alone, this
first time.

Briony was feeling rather shy as she went to the hospital, but she soon forgot that when eventually she was shown into the little side room where Miss Lomax lay. Miss Lomax smiled when she saw her visitor, and held out her hand.

"Well, Briony Hunter," Miss Lomax said. "Thanks to you and your commendably quick thinking, I am still in the land of the living. I'm extremely grateful to you—there! Now you have gone as red as one of my peonies!"

"Oh dear," said Briony; suddenly remembering.

"What is it?"

"I was going to bring you some flowers," Briony confessed. "And I quite forgot. I'm so sorry. There isn't anything else that I can give you."

"Hmph!" said Miss Lomax. "You've given me my life, child. I think that will do nicely for one week! But sit down, do. You look as though you have been asked, but couldn't come!"

Briony giggled, and obediently sat down.

"How are you feeling? I should have asked before."

Miss Lomax gave one of her dry chuckles.

"Not used to being a hospital visitor, are you? And a refreshing change, if I may say so. I've been asked how I feel till I'm tired! How is

Ginger Bob? And how did you manage to rescue me?"

"Ginger Bob's settling quite well. But I'm feeling rather squirmy about how we rescued you," Briony confessed. "You see, I kept trying to see you, and you didn't answer. And all the doors were locked—I'm afraid I tried them—and I saw the plants in the greenhouse were wilting, so I *knew* something was wrong. So we—well—we— broke in!"

Miss Lomax made a most peculiar noise, rather like a cough and a chuckle mixed up together. Briony eyed her uncertainly. It was surely nothing to *laugh* about, was it? But Miss Lomax was speaking again.

"And how did you manage the housebreaking?"

"Er—with a screwdriver. I got in at the window by the back door. And I broke a saucer," she added. But Miss Lomax did not seem worried about the saucer.

"Child, I can only say 'Thank you' to you— and your friends—but I hope you will know how very heart-felt that is. And I hope to meet your friends another day, and thank them, too."

"They'd like that. I've told them about you and your lovely garden, so they feel they know you a bit. But they'd like to know you properly,"

Briony said. "And they asked me to tell you that they hoped you would soon be quite better. And is there anything we could do for you now?"

"There are a few things I need from End House. I wonder if you would mind bringing them in for me? I'll give you a key; the doctor brought one in, gave one to the police in case of need, and he has another. No need for you to crawl through the window this time!"

Briony grinned in response to the twinkle in her eyes, and put the list and the key safely in her bag. Then she stood up.

"I'll do that gladly, and I'll water the plants every day. But I will come again tomorrow."

Even her inexperienced eyes could see that Miss Lomax was both tired and weak now, so she bent down, put a quick, shy kiss on the pale cheek and slipped out. As she passed through the main ward, she heard someone saying

". . . that must be the little girl who saved the old lady's life," and her cheeks burned.

When she reached home, after a refreshing quick tea with Heather and Jessamy, her mother listened quietly to all she had to tell of her visit, and then, when Briony explained that there were things which Miss Lomax wanted from her home, suggested that Briony changed into her jeans. "I'll take you as far as Cypress House, darling, leave you there to water the plants, and then I'll go to the hospital and take the things which Miss Lomax asked for, and then collect you on my way home."

So this was what they did and Mrs. Hunter willingly went to the hospital, where she reiterated Briony's statement that they were all glad to help in any way that they could. The ward sister was glad to see her, but Miss Lomax was almost overwhelmed ". . . by your kindness, after all your little girl has already done."

That was the beginning of daily visits to the hospital. Either Mr. Hunter or Mrs. Hunter went each day, and sometimes they went together in the evening. It was on one of these occasions that Miss Lomax felt sufficiently at ease with them to explain herself a little, and the Hunters passed it on to their elder children when the twins were in bed.

"It's a sad story, Bri, and I hope that things will be better for Miss Lomax now. We're going to treat you and Mark as responsible people by telling you all this, remember, so although Miss Lomax doesn't mind you knowing, she won't want you gossiping idly. And I hope it will help you to remember how lucky you are."

"Go on, then," Mark urged. "What happened to her?"

"Miss Lomax was one of a big family, as Briony has told us. In those days, it wasn't usual for girls to have careers as they do now. They stayed at home until it was time for them to marry and have homes of their own."

"Not all of them," Mark objected. "I mean, we hear quite a bit these days of the ones who went out as servants."

"Yes, that's true. But girls whose families were a bit more wealthy didn't, and the Lomaxes were quite well off, without being rich. Miss Lomax's sister Lydia was married when she was quite young and so Miss Lomax was left as the daughter of the house; helping her mother with entertaining and so on. Then a dreadful thing happened. Mrs. Lomax was killed out hunting and her husband was so upset that he had what would now be called a heart-attack, and within two days of his wife, he had died, too.

"Naturally, all the children were dreadfully upset, but it affected Bri's Miss Lomax the most, for Lydia was married and away in London, and then war was declared—the First World War—and all three boys went into the army—they were an army family."

"Oh, *don't* say they were all killed!" Briony implored, nearly in tears. "Not *all* of them!"

"They weren't all killed in action, Bri," Mrs.

Hunter said gently. "You must realise that medicine wasn't like it is now, and that conditions in war-time are always difficult."

"You mean that they died of—well—fever and bad conditions and that sort of thing? I've read about it," Mark said, and his mother nodded.

"I'm afraid so, Mark. Derek died that way and Roger died from wounds which were never properly treated. And the Lomax girls were just recovering from that blow when there was another, for Bernard, the youngest of the family and our Miss Lomax's favourite—was killed on his twentieth birthday."

Briony's eyes filled, and her brother kicked the chair opposite and said gruffly:

"Rotten. I don't wonder the old lady felt that nothing was worthwhile."

"She didn't—then. She kept up a normal life, happy in her old home. And she had become very interested in gardening, and there was plenty to do there, and in helping people in her village. And Bri will perhaps understand this better than you, but Miss Lomax said she believed that through everything she had the friendship of God to cling to."

"I do understand," said Briony. "And what changed that?"

"A mixture of a lot of things, Briony. Old

quarrels with village people that were never made up. Disagreements at church—and bad feeling that was allowed to go on and on. Miss Lomax didn't tell me all her reasons, but I think perhaps the thing which made her finally withdraw was when her sister Lydia, Lydia's husband and their two sons—all of whom she loved dearly—were killed when a bomb destroyed their home in the Second World War. So she had no one.

"Now, I don't know if you two will understand this now, but I hope you will as you get older. People are all different, and they react in different ways. Some people, when they are very unhappy, go out to their friends and allow themselves to be comforted. But some people, although they desperately want and need love and care, go right inside themselves and shut other people out. They can't help it; it's just like an illness. But this is what people don't understand. This is what happened to Miss Lomax."

"I say!" Mark said soberly. "It makes you think, doesn't it? I mean—people would probably offer to help at first, but I don't expect they would go on. And if Miss Lomax was still ill and upset, she would think they didn't want to—and there would be a deadlock."

"Quite right," Mr. Hunter agreed. "That is exactly what happened. And after a while, the enforced loneliness became a habit. And so things went from bad to worse—until Briony came along and hung over the wall of Cypress House to admire the garden."

"So she's some use, after all!" Mark said cheerfully, and Briony gave him an indignant swipe, until she realised that it was just his way of lightening the atmosphere after the sad story which they had heard.

"But it wasn't really me who helped," she insisted, when they were calm again. "It was Jesus. *He* kept telling me there was something wrong, so that I simply *had* to see Miss Lomax, even if it did mean breaking in. And I was simply terrified, although I did it, because I knew that if Miss Lomax *had* been all right, she would have been very angry."

"Well, she wasn't—and she wasn't," Mark said, and they all laughed. "Is that why you told the newspaperman the same?" for the reporter from the local paper had turned up with a photographer, and had insisted on interviewing Briony, who, in her turn, had insisted on roping in her two friends, saying that they had done as much to help as *she* had. Shy Heather had been furious, but Jessamy had taken it all very much in her stride and had talked as though she gave press interviews every week, to the amusement of Mrs.

Hunter, who had insisted on being present. But all three had told their interviewer very firmly that it was the Lord Jesus who had helped them and told them what to do.

"At least Bri isn't the swollen-headed kind," Mr. Hunter said later, with a grin, as he put down the paper. "I say, you do realise that we can't have the puppy this weekend, don't you? We can't risk upsetting Ginger Bob now he has settled down, and it will only be for another couple of days or so. By the way, I've told Dr. Meadows that one of us will go in to Cypress House every day to make sure that Miss Lomax is all right, and he and the district nurse will call as well, so with Bri and her pals running in and out, Miss Lomax should find life a little less lonely when she does go home."

"And," Mrs. Hunter added quietly, "I think that article in the paper did at least one good piece of work, for it gave the village a nasty shock. If Bri hadn't gone—well, it would have been a real tragedy. The vicar was very chastened when he spoke to me in the hospital, and says that he has had a sharp lesson about letting people alone. I gather he has told people at church the same. And now that Miss Lomax has agreed to have help in the house—which she wouldn't have done if the doctor hadn't insisted, and even *then* they argued for half an hour!—that nice Mrs. Rogers is going in. And I'm sure she gets all the village gossip, so Miss Lomax should be well and truly drawn back in. Not a bad ending, after all!"

This was very much what Briony and her friends were saying as they walked slowly away from Cypress House a few days later, for Miss Lomax had insisted that they must be her first visitors when she got home.

"This has been a jolly exciting summer," Briony said. "First moving here, and our new house, and then meeting you and getting to know Jesus and all that.

"Then meeting Miss Lomax, and starting to make my own garden, and then that awful night which seems to have done some good. And to-morrow we get our puppy, and then——"

"—school begins!" said Jessamy mischievously, and Briony pulled a face.

"I could do without that, I must say! But even that won't be so bad, because there will be you and Heather. And Mother says I can start going to Bible Class with you. So, although I'm sorry the summer's over, I'm sure there will be plenty of interesting things to come."

And she was right. But that is another story.